suck
it in
and
smile

Published in English in Canada and the USA in 2022 by Groundwood Books
Translation copyright © 2022 by Shelley Tanaka
Original title: *Rentrer son ventre et sourire*
Originally published in French (Canada)
Copyright © by Éditions de la Bagnole, Montreal, Canada, 2020

Groundwood Books / House of Anansi Press
groundwoodbooks.com

We gratefully acknowledge for their financial support of our publishing program the
Canada Council for the Arts, the Ontario Arts Council and the Government of Canada.

 Canada Council
for the Arts   Conseil des Arts
du Canada

 ONTARIO ARTS COUNCIL
CONSEIL DES ARTS DE L'ONTARIO
an Ontario government agency
un organisme du gouvernement de l'Ontario

 With the participation of the Government of Canada
Avec la participation du gouvernement du Canada   Canadä

Library and Archives Canada Cataloguing in Publication
Title: Suck it in and smile / Laurence Beaudoin-Masse ; translated by Shelley Tanaka.
Other titles: Rentrer son ventre et sourire. English
Names: Beaudoin-Masse, Laurence, author. | Tanaka, Shelley, translator.
Description: Translation of: Rentrer son ventre et sourire.
Identifiers: Canadiana (print) 20210390662 | Canadiana (ebook) 20210390670 |
ISBN 9781773068091 (paperback) | ISBN 9781773068107 (EPUB)
Classification: LCC PS8603.E33678 R4613 2022 | DDC jC843/.6—dc23

Printed and bound in Canada

MIX
Paper from
responsible sources
FSC
www.fsc.org   FSC® C103567

suck
it in
and
smile

WRÍTTEN BY
Laurence
Beaudoin-Masse

TRANSLATED BY SHELLEY TANAKA

Groundwood Books
House of Anansi Press
Toronto / Berkeley

GOALS

When I was a teenager, I spent more time dreaming my life than I did living it. The reality was just so... unpleasant. So I would daydream a lot — during class, on the bus, before I fell asleep. I imagined having a boyfriend who thought I was beautiful. Marks that made my parents proud. People to eat with in the cafeteria. A talent — any talent...

But I had none of that. I would have changed places with anyone. I would have given anything just to stop being me. I've spent so many years doing everything I can to be less like me. To become someone else.

I thought one day things would get easy.

If you only knew how much effort, starvation and hard work I inflicted on myself to get where I am. To be in the top ten of the most popular YouTubers. To have 250,000 followers on Instagram. Body goals. Couple goals. Life goals.

Everything was going so well. I told myself that I was finally That Girl.

But I didn't understand a thing. Nothing at all.

And it wouldn't take long for it all to hit me right in the face.

1

I still have brain mush and gummy eyes when I get to the bathroom. I grab the toothbrush and toothpaste, and all of a sudden it hits me.

It's September 13th.

I have been officially going out with Samuel Vanasse for nine months.

A thrill of joy rushes through me, right from my toenails to the tips of my eyelashes.

My life has taken a turn so incredibly, fabulously, monumentally wonderful lately that I've developed this strange habit. I bite the inside of my cheek to make sure I'm not dreaming. A dream so excruciatingly sensational that just waking up would make me want to curl up in my bed for all eternity.

I hold my breath. I bite down hard so I'll really feel it.

It hurts. I'm reassured.

I'm brushing my teeth when Sam walks into the bathroom, pointing the camera of his iPhone at me.

"What are you doing?"

"I'm making a story."

Sam gives me his cute little smile. The one that

makes him look like a little kitten, but manly.

I blush. He moves behind me, films us both in the mirror with him holding me around the waist. He nuzzles my cheek with his nose. It tickles.

I gather what little concentration I have left.

"Stop it, no…I'm in my pajamas and I'm brushing my teeth."

"Gorgeous. Instagram is going to crash."

"Hardly! You'll just lose a ton of followers. Not that it matters. You don't have that many anyway."

"Uh, I have at least 50,000, you know."

"Cute! That's about 200,000 less than me."

"Ouch."

I burst out laughing. Sam finally puts his iPhone down on the sink. I barely have time to rinse my toothbrush before he grabs me by the shoulders and pulls me to him.

Pressed against Sam, I'm like a melted marshmallow. We kiss. Our hair gets all tangled. Our tongues, too. He lifts me up and throws me over his shoulder.

I kick and laugh as he carries me to his room. He puts me down on the bed and starts kissing my neck.

Out of the corner of my eye, I look at the time: 10:42 a.m.

I'm late.

"I want to, but I don't have time."

Sam makes a sound halfway between a growl and a sigh.

"Stay, Ellie."

"I can't, baby. I'm having lunch with my sister."

"No, stay here. Live with me."

Three little words that feel like an explosion of confetti in my belly.

"Are you serious?"

"Never been so serious in my life."

I jump on top of him.

"I have ten minutes, but no more."

Top 10 YouTubers
CAN/FR

1. Jordanne Jacques – 802,550 followers
2. Tellement Cloé – 760,340 followers
3. Emma & Juju – 506,900 followers
4. Cath Bonenfant – 500,370 followers
5. Mila Mongeau – 498,110 followers
6. **Ellie – Quinoa Forever – 495,300 followers**
7. Approved by Gwen – 421,400 followers
8. Sophie Chen – 340,700 followers
9. Maëla Djeb – 160,260 followers
10. Zoé around the World – 142,290 followers

TEAM ELLIE

When I started Quinoa Forever about two years ago, I had the best of intentions. My goal was to inspire girls to be the best version of themselves.

At the time, it was nothing but a little side project. I had just lost a lot of weight. I'd changed my lifestyle, my diet, my way of being...You could almost say that I had become a new person. And that was, among other things, thanks to American YouTubers like Ella Austin or Becky Robins, who had their own way of being inspiring and accessible. Thanks to their Instagram feeds, which made me want to make my own oat milk or picnic in a lavender field. I got off on their lives. On their videos. I didn't understand why there was nothing like that here in Quebec.

So I decided to do it.

I didn't expect things to take off so fast. I still have a little trouble believing it.

My agent says there are two kinds of big-time influencers. I'm not talking about people who become popular because of their reality TV shows or who are already famous. I'm talking about true influencers.

There are the ones who have worked hard for

their success, who fight for every follower and who keep fighting their way to the top. Then there are the ones who become an overnight success and you can never really explain how. A combination of timing and luck, I guess.

I belong to the second category. I kind of got popular by accident. People glommed onto me right away.

My agent says that the danger in cases like mine is that the fall into oblivion can be as fast as the rise to glory. Because we didn't have to work very hard to succeed, we haven't developed good reflexes.

We think it's always going to be this easy, but the real challenge is to last.

2

By the time I get to the Vv Café, I'm a complete disaster. I'm at least half an hour late. My sister, Alice, is sitting in front of a latte the size of a wading pool. Her nose is plunged into a copy of *The Social Construction of Reality.* She chews on her thumbnail as she frantically highlights important passages.

Much to my mother's despair, Alice has just started a second degree. After three years in philosophy and a semester in law, she's finally decided that sociology is her thing. And it's true that she has no trouble succeeding at school. She's super talented, but totally blasé about it, plus she's a world-class party animal. Alice's life is one big cycle of "party-hard evening followed by a rough morning and an intensive phase of recovery."

I've become an expert at judging how intense her evening has been based on what she looks like after she wakes up.

This morning it's an ironic Powerpuff Girls T-shirt, messy bun, clouds of mascara under her eyes and a supersize coffee.

At first glance, I would say four hours' sleep and

a three-out-of-five-grade headache.

She rolls her eyes when she sees me.

"Seriously, of all the places to meet for lunch, this is what you pick? I feel like I'm INSIDE Pinterest right now, and it's scary. Personally, I always choose restaurants that have the word 'Egg' in their name. You can count on the bacon being crisp, and they won't be cheap with those little packs of strawberry jam."

"Good morning, Alice. I'm doing well, thanks for asking. You?"

"As well as a girl who's had four hours of sleep can be doing. I really have to start going to bed early. And before you mention it, yes, I am wearing the same shirt I was wearing last time."

Alice is the kind of girl who doesn't want you to think she cares how she looks. She spends her life wearing way-too-big old rags that she finds at the thrift store.

She's a beautiful girl, my sister. She just doesn't want anyone to be interested in her for that reason.

She throws an impatient look at the server. Then she looks at me for the first time since I arrived. I can tell that she's studying me closely.

She frowns. "What's with the face? You look like you just saw a unicorn."

"Almost! Brace yourself, because I'm going to —"

"You're finally going to introduce me to your hot agent."

"What? Malik? No. You think he's hot?"

"Have you slept with him yet?"

"Alice! He's my agent."

"Exactly. It's the perfect erotic scenario."

"What are you talking about?! No, what's happened is that I'm going to mo —"

Right in the middle of my big announcement, the server arrives to ask if we're ready to order. I haven't even looked at the menu yet, but Alice, who obviously doesn't care about that, jumps at the chance.

While she's busy ordering the Hungry Man special with extra sausage, I quickly scan the menu.

Scones, that's a billion calories. Waffles, hello sugar. Bagels, forget it. Breakfast poutine? Overrated, frankly. What's next, shepherd's pie with hollandaise sauce? Gross.

Maybe they have a fruit platter? Nope. I should have looked up the menu before I came.

The server is getting impatient.

"Uh...I'm...going to have the breakfast salad with no bacon, poached eggs not fried, dressing on the side, brown bread with no butter and a large chai tea. Not the latte, just tea."

The server looks at me, amused, picks up the menus and heads to the kitchen.

Alice just stares at me.

"Come on! That's not a meal. It's like eating a fistful of lawn. Even a rabbit would get depressed staring at that plate."

I'd like to explain, but every time I try to tell Alice about my meal planning, it's a disaster. She gets carried away, gives me a lecture, and then I get mad.

I cut the discussion short. "I don't like bacon, and they always put on too much dressing."

"Yeah, right. Don't you think you've lost enough weight already? Seems you could give yourself a break."

"Don't worry about me, okay? I have a nutrition coach. It's all legit."

"Yeah...I still can't believe you pay someone to tell you what to eat. Seriously, when does this diet end?"

"It's not a diet. It's a healthy lifestyle."

"It's not healthy! You're worse than Estelle."

"Since when do you call her Estelle?"

"Ever since she failed miserably to satisfy the minimum requirements for motherhood."

"Don't you think you're exaggerating just a bit?"

"No."

I breathe out a very long sigh, at the end of which I remember what I was trying to tell her before the whole bacon mini-drama.

"So, what I was going to tell you is —"

"Oh, right, I'm listening."

"I'm moving in with Sam. He just asked me. Can you believe it?!"

Alice plunges a spoonful of sugar into the foam of her coffee.

"Oh … hey, that's great," she says without looking up from her cup.

"That's it?"

"How do you want me to react? Ellie, you haven't even been together for six months."

"Nine months, Alice, if you count from our first date. Come on, you're so boring in the morning!"

"No, really, I'm happy for you. But you know me. Not really into the Prince Charming thing. But if you're happy, I'm happy."

I feel like Alice is making a sincere effort to swallow her cynicism, which is pretty rare. Either way, I can hardly blame her for her lack of enthusiasm. Her own love life is kind of pathetic.

"You're an asshole," I say.

"I love you too, Ellie."

The server places our plates on the table.

Alice was right. My breakfast salad looks depressing.

My sister dips her potatoes in ketchup.

"Hey!" she exclaims with her mouth full of egg and baked beans. "My roommates are throwing a party next Saturday. You have to come. It's for my birthday. You can even bring the famous Samuel Vanasse and his abs of steel if you want."

"Abs of steel?"

"I read it in *Celebrity World*."

"You read *Celebrity World*?"

"It happens. Sometimes. Rarely. But don't tell anyone."

"Mmmhmmm."

"Ellie, please! I have a certain reputation to maintain at the university."

"Promise. But I'm stealing your potatoes."

"Deal."

@ELLIE_QUINOA_FOREVER

- A photo of me in a bathing suit on the beach. I'm looking down at the ground. I arch my lower back slightly so my butt sticks out.
- A photo of my face. I'm wearing lipstick. I smile.
- A photo with my boyfriend in the rainforest. My arms around his neck. He's carrying me in his arms. We kiss.
- Figs, almonds and oatmeal.
- My silhouette against a sunset. My arms in the air.
- In a field, I wear a flowered dress and a wool jacket. I'm looking over my shoulder.
- A video. Protein breakfast inspiration.
- A close-up of my sweater with the words Rise Up on it.
- A colorful salad and a glass of water.
- My feet at the edge of the ocean.
- Leaning on a kitchen table, my legs crossed. With one hand I lift the bottom of my dress; in the other I hold a bottle of shampoo.
- Yoga. A sun salutation.
- With my boyfriend in profile in a crowd. He cradles my left leg in his right hand. My arms around his

neck. Our noses touch as we gaze into each other's eyes.

- In bed, I'm sleeping on my side. The blanket is placed so you can just see the curve of my buttocks and the cleavage of my breasts.
- A photo of me at age three.
- My boyfriend holds me around the waist. I'm putting an energy ball in his mouth. I'm laughing.
- I'm holding a basket of apples. Nail polish on my fingers.
- A close-up of my face. I'm staring at the camera.
- A bouquet of flowers from my lover.
- My living room. I light a candle. In my panties. I'm wearing a wool sweater.
- Autumn leaves. I'm doing a plank, resting on my forearms.
- A video of my boyfriend playing the guitar. He's in his pajamas.
- A hammock. Warm socks. My bare legs.
- Me in front of a white brick wall. I'm wearing pink shorts and doing a squat.
- Video. Three must-do stretches before going to bed.
- Me in front of a bowl of soup. My cheek resting in my hand.

- Orange wedges on a wooden board. Sprigs of rosemary. A jar of vitamins.
- I'm running in a park. I look straight ahead. My breasts rise up in the air along with my right leg.
- Sitting cross-legged on my kitchen counter, I eat yogurt. I'm wearing leggings. I'm laughing.
- A bowl filled with strawberries. A wooden spoon. Some plant-based milk.
- Sitting on the edge of a dock, my legs stretched out. I'm wearing sneakers. I hold a green smoothie in one hand. I play with my hair with the other.
- Avocado toast. A cup of tea.
- In a mirror, my boyfriend kissing me on the neck.
- A video on the importance of breathing well.
- A tree silhouetted against a sunrise.
- An umbrella in hand, a flowered skirt, I wink, I smile.

INFLUENCE

If there's one thing that annoys influencers, it's being told that they are influencers. In general, we prefer to be known as "content creators." I would never say this in front of my colleagues, but I think it's hilarious to talk about our work this way. I mean, it's so deliberately...vague. As if a large part of what we do isn't exerting our influence over our followers.

For sure there are many different kinds of influencers. I totally understand that a girl like Chloé Rioux, who built her career by making kickass videos of herself taking on crazy challenges, would not want to be put in the same category as an Insta-babe who earns her living getting plastic surgery, or some chick who just shares unboxing videos at #gifted. I don't want to be associated with those girls, either. And it's true that creating good content is a big part of my job.

But I wonder if it isn't a bit hypocritical to pretend that we're just "content creators" and nothing else.

You know, I won't deny that even with millions of views, advertising income from my YouTube videos amounts to, what — a few hundred dollars a month? Sometimes it's a lot more, other times a lot less. Not enough to live on, that's for sure. But ever since my channel became popular I get tons of partnership offers. Brands pay me to talk about their products on Instagram or in my videos. This is how I earn my living. I sell makeup, yogurt, coffee, yoga clothes, shampoo, supplements, glasses, sneakers — you name it.

That's why the expression "content creator" makes me laugh. I mean, you're kidding, right? That would be, like, the difference between me and a photographer. Technically we're both "content creators." She takes pictures and I make videos, right? Yet you'd never hear a photographer call herself a content creator. She's a photographer because what she sells is her pictures.

But what am I selling? My content? No. What I sell is the people who watch my videos. What brands want when they hire me is to reach my audience. I sell my influence. I am an influencer.

We're not going pretend otherwise, are we?

QUINOA FOREVER

I am so happy to FINALLY be able to reveal to you my top secret project!!!

I've written a book! It's called *Radiant*. Inside you'll find small happiness tips, exercise routines (which you will actually want to do, I promise) and a ton of detox recipes. As a bonus, I'll tell you how I learned to be my own best friend and how that has changed my life.

Coming out in bookstores on November 30! I sincerely hope you like it. ❤ ❤ ❤

To preorder, click here. ❤ Ellie XX

👍❤😮 **Mélodie Leclerc and 7.3 K others** - 482 comments - 41 shares

Catherine Nantel OMG! Can't wait to buy it. I adore your recipes ❤ ❤ ❤ #TeamEllie

Andréa Lou You are so inspiring. Thank you for being there and KALE POWER (lol).

Lea Mourman Ellie, everything you do is awesome! Thanks for all the advice and ideas. You've changed my life so much. I'm about to reach my goal. I can't believe it, I'd never have got there without you!!! (I'm speaking for myself, but I think everyone feels the same way.) Anyway, I love you, you're so cool. #TeamEllie

Sophie Sophie I can't handle this chick. To be your best friend lol. I wouldn't want to.

Lilas Morissette Ellie if you see this message, can you subscribe to my YouTube channel please? I love you so much, hugs.

Samu_elle Have you gained weight? Maybe throw out a challenge, 10 pounds before Christmas!!! Plz!

Camille Bastien-Bernier Yippeeee! **@soraya_millano** It's like my birthday, but early!

Show all 475 other comments

3

I have an appointment with Malik, my agent at B-COZ, for our monthly planning session.

It's Jean-Félix, his assistant slash receptionist slash any other related task, who greets me. He takes care of the schedules, writes contracts and follows up. Malik is the one who negotiates fees, works to develop new partnerships and builds my strategy. We meet every month to go over my stats and make a game plan. We set goals for acquisitions, retention, audience growth. We determine how to position me in the market, what I agree to do, what I refuse, what kind of content I'm going to produce — all that. Malik gives his point of view, but I always have the last word.

In exchange, the agency takes a percentage of my income. The arrangement suits me perfectly.

Jean-Félix leads me to Malik's office.

"You can wait for him here. Do you want anything? An espresso?"

"Uh, no thanks, Jean-Fé. I've cut out caffeine."

"You're kidding. You're a saint! I don't know how you do it. All that healthy living, I love it. It must be wild being you! And going out with Samuel Vanasse too. Wow. Is it true that he shaves his armpits?! Hey, sorry, I'm rambling. I'll leave you alone. You must find it exhausting. Sorry, sweetie. I'm going now!"

Jean-Fé rushes off before I can say a word.

I'm alone in the huge glass room. Around me there's a desk, a laptop, a phone, a chair — and silence. No music, no plants, no papers lying around.

It's almost scary. For a second I think about looking in the drawers to see what Malik keeps away from prying eyes. I wonder what I'd find.

In fact, I wonder whether Malik likes me. I mean, whether he appreciates me. Am I just a regular client for him, or does he think I'm special? Kind, talented. Like, his favorite.

I have no clue. He's been managing my career for about a year, but... I have absolutely no idea.

When we first started working together, Malik and I set out to make me one of the top three most popular YouTubers by Christmas. The problem is that since July, I've been stuck in sixth place on the charts. Every time I gain 5,000 new subscribers, Mila Mongeau, the girl in fifth place, gets 6,000. It's so annoying.

I have three months left to climb to third place, and I have no intention of failing. If I need to put in ten times the effort, I'll do it.

Malik's voice startles me. I stand up and run a hand through my hair to look relaxed. I'm super nervous. As usual.

Malik apologizes for being late, hangs his coat on the back of his chair, checks the time, then presses one of the buttons on his huge office phone. I hear Jean-Fé's voice over the speaker. Malik asks him for a long double espresso, offers me one, which I refuse. He presses another button, then opens his computer and starts to look over my statistics for the past three months.

"How many views?" I ask nervously.

"Six million since July. That's good."

"Completion rate?"

"Good overall. Better than this summer."

The completion rate is the percentage of people who watch the video to the end. The more people watch, the more the YouTube algorithm considers the content to be of high quality and the more likely it is to be discovered by other users. This is why You-Tubers always take ten minutes before revealing whatever big news they have. So we'll watch their video for the longest time possible.

"Audience?" I ask.

"Up 23 percent on YouTube."

"Nice!"

"And a good acquisition peak on Instagram in August."

"My trip to Costa Rica."

"You're going up slightly in the 25 to 34 age group, but your core audience is 13- to 24- year-olds. That's 78 percent of all your views in the last three months."

"Even on my vlogging channel?"

"Even on your vlogging channel." Malik taps the desk with his fingertips. I guess something's bothering him about the stats.

"What's the matter? Shoot."

"Well, 32 percent of all your views still come from 13- to 17-year-olds. That's a lot."

For the past few months, Malik has been talking to me about raising the age of my audience. He wants me to come up with content that's a little less girly. He thinks I'd have better commercial opportunities that way.

I thought about it. I even tried to go to 25 to

34, whatever that means, but clearly things haven't changed much.

"It's okay, though, right? The important thing is to have views."

"Ellie, you're going to be twenty-six this year. You're getting older, but your audience isn't growing old with you. It's a problem. You can't keep selling lip gloss and acne cream forever. That's without even considering the purchasing power of 25- to 34-year-olds, which is a lot better than teenagers."

"Yes, I understand," I say, a little discouraged. "You're right, but..."

Malik puts down his phone, and his eyes meet mine.

"Listen, I've been thinking about this a lot, Ellie. And I think part of the problem is that you're trying too hard to be perfect."

"Um. Okay."

"Do you see what I'm talking about?"

"Not really."

"I love your content and think it appeals to girls your age, but in my opinion, it's a question of personality. You're, like..."

"Fake?"

"No, no, not at all! You are like the slightly annoying girl at the top of the class."

"Oh. Okay."

"Don't take it badly...but my feeling is that girls your age — they don't want to be your friend. They want to watch you trip over your sneakers and fall face first into your kale muffins."

"..."

"I'm not going to ask you to be trashy and sexy like a Cath Bonenfant or a Maëla Djeb. You don't have it in you. And that's fine. I think that you should be shown in a more nuanced light. More mature, more...womanly."

"More womanly?"

"Well, listen, if we let the stats speak for themselves, we see, for example, that the 25 to 34's loved your trip to Costa Rica with Sam. People love to see you two together and in love on the beach."

"Okay, so when Sam puffs out his chest, I look like a woman. Is that it?"

"No...But it's good to see you through the eyes of the people who love you. Sam is great leverage for your career. Your audience loves it!"

Malik talks about Sam pretty much every time we

see each other. Frankly, it's starting to get annoying. It's true that my posts with him perform well. Better than average, even. And I'm happy about that, so I keep doing it, but that can't be my strategy. That can't be the point of my channel.

My goal has always been to help girls feel good about themselves, to eat better and move more. I don't see what my musician boyfriend has to do with it.

"But, Malik, if I want to be in the top three by Christmas, this is hardly the time to change my strategy, is it?"

"I don't think we'll get there any other way. The fact is that you're still stuck in sixth place."

I sigh. I must look a little put out, because Malik adds, "Trust me, Ellie. I am never wrong."

I promise I'll think about it.

I sink back in my chair. Malik is probably right, but the truth is, it annoys me. Seems like even when things are going okay there's always something that I should be doing differently. It's never enough.

"I just need a little time to . . . take it all in."

"Good, Ellie, good."

Malik checks the time, then gives me a big smile.

He presses one of the buttons on his phone and asks Jean-Félix to bring in his next guest.

"I have a little surprise for you!"

"A surprise?!"

I sit up in my chair, excited. I like surprises. I love them! I wonder what it is.

I subtly try to add a little volume to my hair, and I run my tongue over my teeth.

Maybe a gift for my 250,000 followers on Instagram? You never know.

"The team came up with an idea…"

A blonde girl walks into the office. I recognize her right away.

It's Mila Mongeau. The YouTuber. The one who's just ahead of me on the Top Ten list.

But I don't just know her because of that.

We went to high school together. Our relationship was…complicated.

Let's say that like a lot of people at the time, Mila liked to make fun of me behind my back. Except it wasn't just that. We had a kind of falling out in our final year.

Anyway, there's no point going over this.

Now Mila does DIY and lifestyle videos. I admit

that she does have some talent. She even launched her own collection of decorative accessories in collaboration with XY Home. I find that pretty impressive.

"Ellie," Malik says proudly, "may I present your new BFF! Mila has just joined the agency."

"..."

"So, rather than seeing yourselves as rivals, we thought you could be collaborators!"

I force myself to smile at Mila. She holds out her hand.

"Collaborators?" I say.

"Yes. Friends. Make videos together. Mila will give you a hand attracting the 25- to 34-year-olds, and in exchange, you can give her a little visibility on Instagram. I think you both have a lot to gain from partnering up."

"Yeah, that's nice," I say quickly, "but —"

"Nice to meet you, Ellie." Mila cuts me off.

I freeze.

There is no way Mila has forgotten me. No. Way. I don't know why she's pretending we don't know each other.

"Listen, Ellie," Malik says. "I'm really sorry, but we're going to have to say goodbye. We have a conference call with LA in two minutes. But I'll set up a meeting right away to discuss all this. Nothing is set in stone! Let's meet and then we'll see. And in the meantime, if you have any questions, you can call Jean-Fé!"

"Uh, sure. Thanks."

"Okay, great meeting. You're doing good work. See you soon!" Malik waves and I wave back. I gather up my things in a bit of a rush and leave his office.

Mila is glued to her phone and pays no attention to me.

It's only when I get to the end of the hall in front of reception that I realize the extent of the disaster that has just occurred.

Because — in case it isn't already clear — the fact is that Mila and I hate one another.

THROWBACK

It may be hard to believe now, but from between age eleven and twenty-one, I was obese. Truly.

At the time, there was a very popular scientific calculation for it. The body mass index.

BMI = weight divided by height squared.

Mine was over thirty. Which doctors and the world in general seemed to find problematic.

As for me, to be honest, before I was eleven or so, I didn't pay much attention to my body or realize it was different. It could laugh, walk, sleep, think, digest food, bend and stretch…

I didn't feel like I was "sick" or abnormal. Except when it came time to shop for clothes.

Shopping was complicated. Everything was too small. To my dismay, my mother would take me to the women's department of her favorite department store. She chose corduroy pants, wool skirts, turtle-necks and knit jackets. We had to adjust the seams, roll up the sleeves, take up the hems. I looked like Miss Marple reincarnated as a grade-school student. To the point that my friends would ask me why I dressed like the teachers.

Then one day I outgrew the ladies' sizes and had to go to a special store. A store with "plus" in the name. Plus more fabric maybe, more floral patterns definitely, but not more style.

I would have given everything to be able to dress like my friends. To wear normal clothes.

Then I was thirteen, and a lot of things got complicated. Starting with love. I never had a boyfriend in high school. Not even close. At school, I was always on the C-list. Never the A-list. Not even B. The guys I had a crush on were always more interested in my friends. I existed, but I did not exist.

I would have given anything to have a boyfriend. Anything to be thought of as attractive.

Mila Mongeau, on the other hand, was not only one of the prettiest girls in school, she had a boyfriend and she was an exceptional athlete and had a talent for drawing.

It seemed so blatantly unfair to me. She had everything and I had nothing.

I was jealous.

The worst part was that I couldn't even hold it against her. She was nice. At least, I thought she was nice. Before the "incident" in final year, I considered her to be a friend. Once every cycle, we spent the afternoon taking visual arts with Monsieur Latreille.

To my great dismay, I was a walking disaster. Everything I touched turned out looking like a big brown blotch or a big brown blob.

But Mila knew how to do everything. She'd often give me tips to mix my colors or improve my drawings. We chatted. I thought she was dazzling. And I made her laugh. I felt comfortable around her.

Mila was new to art class. She quit the volleyball team at the start of the year. At five-foot-two, she was too short for the senior team. The net was too high. She made costly mistakes. To give her credit, I think she was pretty shaken up about it at the time.

She decided to switch to visual arts, but she continued to hang out with the girls on the volleyball team after class.

That was the problem. A problem with light-brown hair, sculpted biceps and powerful forearms: Ariane Brunelle.

Mila was a thousand times cooler holding a brush than she was when she was hanging out with her star athlete friend. But as soon as we left art class, it was like she didn't know me. When I passed her in the hall, she ignored me completely while Ariane sent me looks full of disdain. I never understood why, but Ariane decided to hate me with a passion.

I was the chosen one.

But, hey, at that point Mila and I were a long way from imagining what was waiting for us at the end of the year.

My stomach hurts just thinking about it.

4

My coach Josiane's office is lined with all kinds of posters. There are new ones at each of my sessions.

At first it was graphics of Canada's Food Guide.

Then there were a ton of motivational phrases:

If it doesn't challenge you, it won't change you.

Apologies don't burn calories.

Be the badass girl today that you were too lazy to be yesterday.

New this month are photos of Josiane dressed in spandex at Ironman Mont-Tremblant.

If Alice ever saw all this "grossophobic propaganda" (her expression, not mine), I would hear about it until the end of time.

Alice is the only person in the world who never congratulated or envied me for losing weight. She says I'm just conforming to "stupid and unhealthy" standards of beauty.

But that's Alice. For me, it helps me stay on track to have a coach. Even though she is a bit...intense.

At each meeting, Josiane weighs me on a super-sophisticated machine. Then she adjusts my diet plan and workout routine.

She pulls my results out of the printer and circles two, three digits with a pink marker before saying, "Sweetie, your DeepBÖDY test indicates a little weight gain, almost nothing. The muscle mass is in good shape, which means that we should talk about your increase in body fat. The good news is that I see you are super hydrated today. This is wow! A girl who is hydrated is a girl who is thriving, big time."

Getting bigger. I hate it. In front of me, Josiane is all smiles.

An overwhelming urge comes over me. I'm thinking of pouring my water bottle over her head. Watching the liquid trickle down in her hair before falling in big drops onto her shoulders.

No. While Josiane fills out my file on the computer, I think about all the times in the past month that I should have abstained from eating. All the workouts I could have done more of, worked longer, harder.

I feel guilty.

"Did you follow your eating strategy?"

"Kind of. But I'm going to get back to it."

In a burst of enthusiasm, Josiane says, "You could set yourself a sports goal to motivate you to make good choices."

"Like what? An extra workout each week?"

"I think you can aim even higher! What is it that spontaneously comes to your mind?"

"Um...run a half marathon?"

"Yes, that would be — WOW!"

I don't take the time to think about it.

"Okay, I'm game," I answer.

"Yes, that's my girl!"

♡ ◯ ↑

23 538 Likes

ellie_quinoa_forever As far back as I can remember I've always wondered if one day I would meet THE ONE. My one and only. My Prince Charming. I never expected that I would find someone even better. Sam challenges me to be the best version of myself. He pushes me to go for it and make my dreams come true. And he does it not because he wants me to be perfect. He does it because he knows what I'm capable of. **@sam_van** you do bring out the best in me. So excited at the idea of moving in with you! I love you. **#lovehim #hestheone #couple #relationships**

See all 111 comments

sam_van ❤❤❤❤

soraya_d You are so beautiful together!! You are made for each other, and I wish you every happiness. Here's to you both!

ladauphinette @olicloutier Yo babe we could be **#goals** too.

veganfit Hot hot hot.

josée_lo I am so happy for you Ellie! You are a wonderful person and you deserve all the happiness in the world. Thank you for motivating us to be the best version of ourselves. **#TeamEllie**

sarahmichelle So happy for both of you! 🖤

luger1301 Yeah, right. I don't believe it for two seconds. The photo is just to show off your boyfriend's pecs, because that's all he's got.

mj.blouin Wow. The best couple ever in my eyes.

honorable.41 @antoinelambert4 Check it out so beautiful.

erikamajeau You are so cute!

jimenamena Perfect.

vlamontagne It's so so cuuuuute. You are the most beautiful couple on IG.

vero_vero_vero Wow you are too beautiful together.

elementsbarresports Such a good looking couple.

roseamanda This picture is on fire!

isallo #fakelove for sure. Otherwise you wouldn't need to show off all the time.

shophie22 YOU ARE TOO BEAUTIFUL. **#TeamEllie**

vancharette I love your love.

caro_jpeg Need help unpacking?

westmtl Hello **@ellie_quinoa_forever** Can we share your photo on our page, please?

karineflo I don't think he's into you. He doesn't look like he's in love with you. You're just a cover for him.

5

I waited three days to seem independent. Then I sublet my apartment and started to take my boxes over to Sam's place.

His condo has lots of potential, but it needs a LOT of love. Sam's the kind of guy who stores his hockey gear in the cupboard above the fridge and who considers his music instruments to be items of home decor.

In other words, there is work to be done to make it beautiful, and so I can shoot my videos from all angles.

This morning, after two days of nonstop work, I finally finished rearranging the kitchen.

I have my nose in a cupboard when Sam wanders in and starts rooting around.

"Glad to see that the spices are arranged in alphabetical order."

"I follow the Marie Kondo method. First you take everything out, and then you just put back what brings you joy. What *sparks* joy. If it doesn't, then give it away."

Amused, Sam inspects the kitchen.

"I am reassured to learn that lentils spark joy."

"There you go. Let's hear it for plant proteins!"

"Wow, my apartment is on its way to becoming another success story signed by Ellie."

"Yeah, I've given it everything I've got. And if I can turn around the kitchen this week, it'll be a good start."

I hug Sam. I feel like taking a mini-nap standing in his arms. He gives me a peck on my forehead and goes back to rummaging in the cupboards.

"Where did you put my granola bars? The ones with marshmallow?"

"Uh...haven't seen 'em."

"Impossible. It was a full box. You must have thrown them away."

"No, I'd remember...You can have one of my energy balls if you want."

"The little coconut balls? I already ate them. They're weird."

"It's because of the maca powder. You ate them all?!"

I open the fridge. No trace of my energy balls.

It's a disaster. Not a single healthy snack in sight and my yoga class starts in exactly thirty minutes.

"Sammy, those were my snacks for the whole week!

My coach insists that when I finish a workout, I need a snack that contains carbohydrates AND protein. Otherwise my training is absolutely useless."

Sam doesn't really look like he understands the situation he's put me in.

"Yeah, those things don't really fill you up," he says. "I ate seven or eight of them and I still had to make myself a sandwich after."

"Not with the chicken breast, I hope?"

"Um, yes."

"All of it?"

"Yeah."

"That was for my dinners! Seriously, Sam, if we're going to live together, you can't just go around sabotaging my meal prep like that!"

"I'll be careful, I promise."

Sam puts a hand on his heart. He seems to think this is funny.

I want to keep my cool, but I feel like curling up in bed and crying.

I haven't stopped going for two seconds since the move, and I still took time to do my meal prep last night. I stayed up until 2:00 a.m. to finish it. I absolutely cannot afford to let up on my good habits. Life transitions like moving are really tricky moments. One day you stop paying attention, then it's two days, then, oops, a week...and before you know it, you've lost your rhythm.

"You couldn't have known..." I say.

"It's going to be okay. It's not as if there's no food around here, eh?" Sam points to our brand-new wall of shelves filled with squash, plants and mason jars perfectly labeled and lined up.

I force myself to smile. I'm trying hard to rearrange my meal plan for the week. I'll have to find another lean protein to replace the chicken in my quinoa, kale and cranberry salad. Tofu, maybe? Though I was supposed to make a peanut stir-fry on Tuesday...

Anyway, that's perfect. I have two packages in the freezer...though, too much soy in one week isn't really recommended.

Unless I make a chicken stir-fry instead of the tofu and replace the edamame with snow peas or kidney beans. Okay, that'll work.

I'm getting ready to write this all down in my to-do when Sam puts a hand on my shoulder and says, "If worse comes to worst, couldn't you just skip your snack?"

"Ah shit!" I quickly run through my rows of mason jars. Lentils, chickpeas, brown rice, coconut sugar, ground chia…

Argh, and I don't even have the time to make a smoothie.

Sam's staring at me like a wild turkey has taken control of my body.

"No! I cannot just skip my snack!"

"But it's just yoga…"

"So?"

"Well, maybe you don't need to automatically have a snack after yoga. It's not as if you're doing the Ironman…"

"What? Forget it…My coach says…Just…Never mind."

I'm pissed off, but I'm still smiling.

Shit, I'm late. I grab the jar of chia seeds. I may be able to figure out a way to use them on the way.

Sam pulls me close. He presses his pelvis against my bum.

"I'll make you a big snack tonight. With extra protein."

"Yuck! Creepy. Anyway, tonight's Alice's party. You're coming, right?"

"Uh, after rehearsal, yeah."

"Cool. These things are always boring without you." I kiss Sam, I put the chia seeds in my bag and dash off. "See you soon, you sexy snack."

"I'd prefer big snack, or fancy snack."

"Okay, don't push it!"

LOVE

When I first met Sam, I couldn't believe a guy like him would be interested in a girl like me. That a really handsome and popular guy — a guy who could have any girl — would choose me.

I have to tell you that Sam is one of the top ten Hottest Quebecers of the Year, right up there between Lou Bruneau and Éric Tremblay, that he is a heavenly kisser and composes the most beautiful songs in the world.

I mean, he was a finalist on *The Voice*.

We met in front of a radio studio.

It was early January. I was coming out of an interview, he was going in for a recording. We almost ran into each other.

He recognized me. In fact, we'd already been following each other on Instagram for two or three months. Ever since I wrote to tell him that I liked his last song, "Beautiful Scars." I was listening to it ten times a day.

He answered something nice and followed me in return.

I was so happy. I must have spent two hours

dancing for joy all alone in my living room.

After that, every time I posted something, I wondered if he would like it. I kept frantically checking the stats of all my stories to see whether he'd viewed them. And when he did, it was like my heart had a little party.

I don't even remember what we said to each other at the studio that day. It was really cold out, and I think I made some joke about the windchill. An hour later, he invited me to dinner in a DM. We started dating two days later. I'd never met such an upbeat guy. He's so motivated. He's a thousand watts.

The first time he kissed me I was on cloud nine for at least three days. At first I was obsessed with him. I liked the way he walked, laughed, ate, put on his hat, the way he texted, the way he breathed. Every time I thought about him, it was like I was floating.

Being with Sam was great. Except for one thing.

Wherever we went together, I could feel the jealousy of other girls. I could tell just looking at their faces that they were wondering what was so special about me to be with Samuel Vanasse.

And honestly? I was asking myself the same question. Even I was impressed that I was going out with a popular musician. I'll admit at the time I was known on YouTube at the time, but that's all. I was just starting to gain more mainstream success.

When *Celebrity World* published its first article about us, there were lots of girls who followed me just to send me hate mail. They wrote that I wasn't beautiful enough to be with him. That he deserved better.

It was rough, but I can't complain, because it was good exposure for me. I wouldn't be where I am today if I hadn't met Sam. If he hadn't introduced me to the general public.

I'll never forget the moment he asked me to be his girlfriend. It wasn't long after rumors about us started to circulate. We were at a launch for a new band.

During their set, Sam whispered in my ear, "I feel like we're together...want to make it official?"

I didn't stop to question it for a second. I said yes.

That night I felt like I'd arrived somewhere. With him I was no longer the same person, and I loved that.

With him, everything became possible.

6

I go to yoga with my mom twice a week. This is our mother-daughter bonding time and it allows her to, quote, "Stay young because getting old is just an excuse for ugly people."

Lately, though, I am getting the distinct impression that I'm just a cover. My mother will never admit it, but she clearly has the hots for Nico, one of the teachers. It was subtle at first, and then it got downright out of control.

She only goes to his classes. She's the first to arrive so she gets a spot at the front. Asks way too many unnecessary questions about the poses. And, worst of all, she bought this sexy yoga gear to show off her boobs and her butt.

It's really embarrassing. All the more so because Nico is about my age. Imagine my mother lusting after a man who could be her son. It is totally awkward.

I avoid talking about it to Alice, because it would just give her one more excuse to shut out our mother.

"Namaste. For those of you who are new, my name is Nico. I invite you to choose an intention for your practice this afternoon and place it in your heart."

I'm just in time for class. I had to make a quick stop at the café next door to pick up a post-workout snack. I make my way forward as subtly as possible, which isn't easy given all the water bottles, blankets, straps, blocks and cushions on the floor.

When she sees me, my mother gives me the death stare. I know all too well that she is extremely annoyed by my lateness.

"Élisabeth," she whispers loudly, "you're as punctual as your father. It's very difficult!"

Classic. Every time I do something that annoys her, my mother says I take after my father. Since they've been divorced for eight years and she still calls him "the primate," it's hardly a compliment.

I put on my most fake smile and say in my most zen voice, "Hey. I am placing in my heart my intention to show understanding towards menopausal women."

"I am far from menopausal and you know it."

Nico kneels in front of my mother. He puts one hand on her belly and the other on her solar plexus.

"Pranayama. Breathe in through the belly, breathe out through the chest."

Oh, no. My mother gives herself body and soul

to her yoga breathing. I watch her struggle to moan sensually and I want to disappear.

"Hiiiiiiiiiiiiiiiiiih. Fuuuuuuuuuuuuh."

"Very good, Estelle. Balasana. Child's Pose."

Nico sneaks up behind her and presses firmly on her lower back. With her face crushed into the mat, my mother smiles feverishly.

"Mmmm. Yes, I can feel my hips opening. Fuuuuh."

"Excellent, excellent." Nico is far too devoted a teacher. "Downward Dog. Adho mukha svanasana. Raise those hips a little higher, Estelle. That's it!"

I wonder if he suspects that my mother is using him to engage in these pseudo-athletic erotic moments just to spice up her lonely forty-something life.

Poor guy. If he only knew.

∞

After class, I wait for my mother in the locker room while she discusses the second chakra with Nico.

I've already showered by the time she joins me with a dreamy look on her face and a sparkle in her eye.

I feel bad thinking this, but she's pathetic, pursuing this impossible relationship.

As usual, she takes advantage of our time together to talk to me about Alice.

"Smart as she is, your sister could do much better than waste her time on the soft sciences. And she knows it. Your father and I have already paid for one degree. That's enough."

My mother belongs to that generation of women who have no modesty in the locker room. She undresses like it's the most natural thing in the world to be yakking away while standing there completely naked in flipflops.

"She's going to have to understand that at her age, you have to stop relying on mommy and daddy to fulfill your every wish. Going to university is not a life project. Look at you, you're successful in spite of everything."

"In spite of what??"

I always feel funny seeing my mother naked. For lots of reasons. Starting with the fact that when I was a teenager, my mother had a better body than I did. It's a weird feeling to be less thin than your mother. To be less beautiful than your mother. Less desirable than your mother.

Now that I'm an adult and the situation has

changed, I even feel a bit bad for her. My mother may be, as she puts it, "as tight as Robin Wright," but I can't help seeing how hard she's trying to hide it — the passage of time on her body. Her breasts not quite as full, the soft skin on her back, the small wrinkles in her face.

When I look at her, I feel like I've won.

But won what? I don't know.

In my bag, I grab the only edible post-workout snack that I could find on the way: a slice of banana bread.

I'll try to eat just a little bit. The trick is to divide the slice in two and put half of it back right away. Otherwise, it's impossible to stop.

I put the half I don't eat back in its little brown paper bag on the shelf of my locker.

Watching me eat my snack, my mother gives a little jokey laugh.

"You've always loved your dessert!"

She gives me a little tap on my bum. I give her a look that I hope is a bit stern, but not too aggressive. My mother commenting on my diet is not on.

"Come on, muffin, don't be so sensitive! I have a right to make a comment."

"I'm not twelve anymore, Maman. I know what I'm doing. It's important to eat after training. My nutrition coach said so. I made some maca energy balls but Sam ate them."

"You don't have to justify yourself, Élisabeth."

I'm furious. I want to slam the locker door shut, but I'm in a towel with wet hair and a piece of banana bread in my hand. Hardly the time to be making a point.

So I stand there with my snack, feeling guilty.

Meanwhile, my mother finally decides to get dressed. Thank goodness. With my mouth full, I try to pull on my underpants and tights without dropping my towel, but it slips to the floor and I find myself standing there naked, too.

I prefer not to let my mother see me. It's an old reflex.

Moving to hide behind the door of my locker, I step into a puddle of water. My pantyhose get wet.

I'm reaching up to grab my shoes from the top shelf without dropping my banana bread when I feel my mother's gaze on me.

I hold my breath. Suck in my stomach.

My mother is examining me. It's excruciating.

I quickly pick up my towel.

"Okay, I'm going, my big girl. Take care. And try taking it easy on the sweets. You've worked so hard to get to this point. It would be too bad..."

"Bye, Maman."

"Bye, sweetie."

I press my lips together. I have to make an effort to hold back my tears.

My mother sees it. She hurries away.

Dealing with other people's emotions is not really her specialty.

BEAUTIFUL

People like to think I'm superficial. That I'm obsessed with my image because deep down I love myself so much. Admit it. You've thought the same thing yourself about a friend or a girl you follow on Instagram. We like to criticize those who put themselves out there on the internet. We wonder what right they have to expose themselves. They're not that special, right? Certainly not as hot as they think, anyway.

It's true that everyone judges. But have you ever gone so far as to leave a comment? I ask because people send me quite a few...

bilodeaujosianne PLEASE stop thinking you're special. You really aren't that pretty lol.

laurence.mimosa Bitch please, get over yourself.

mikanana Just stop posting. You're still fat FYI. **@jordannejacques** is a thousand times more beautiful than you.

johannepetris I look forward to the day when insignificant bloggers like you stop thinking that what they eat for breakfast is of public interest.

missbjou You have a lovely face, but your thighs are fat. Go and do some squats and stop thinking you're better than everybody else.

I find it ironic that we put so much pressure on women to be beautiful, but then accuse them of being show-offs when they are. Or that we criticize those who value their appearance, but then that's the first thing we attack to put them down.

I admit that being beautiful has become a bit of an obsession with me. Like, one of the most important things.

Is this wrong? You can't deny that life is much easier when you meet the conventional standards of beauty.

I can speak from personal experience. I have clearly already been put in the category of Not Beautiful. Because when you're not thin, people have a hard time seeing your beauty. Worse, they judge you for it. They think if you've failed to manage your appearance, you must be a bit of a loser. That you lack willpower. Because who would choose to look like that? You just need to exercise. You can do it if you want to, right?

But do you really want to know how it happens?

I can't speak for everyone, but for me, it started at the pediatrician's office when I was nine years old. She showed me a small circle that she drew with her pen. This was my weight shown on the normal growth chart for my age.

I was above average.

However, I weighed — what — a few pounds "too much"? Anyway, not a big deal.

Still, they sent me to a nutritionist to teach me how to read the labels on pots of yogurt, calculate the percentage of fat, sugar, calories. They were concerned.

I must be broken. I wasn't growing the way I should.

They started to keep an eye on me. Eating became complicated. Either they would deprive me or I deprived myself, depending on the day. Sometimes I went hungry for hours. My portions were weighed, measured, quantified. I ate in secret. I needed comfort. I looked for it everywhere. I lost control. Food took up all the space in my head. It was both my worst enemy and my best friend.

And because I failed to make my body acceptable in the eyes of others, I came to hate it, too. I got fatter. A lot fatter. Food was my refuge. I wanted to disappear. I was monstrous. I was ashamed of myself.

There was no question of exercising — dancing, jogging. I was ridiculous enough as it was.

I turned thirteen, fourteen, fifteen. I went to a bunch of specialists to get me back to a "normal" weight. I was told I had to lose weight for my health.

But I kept getting bigger. My parents worried.

My weight. A question of health. Really? Instead I got the impression that my body had become the symbol of their parental failure.

I was an embarrassment.

This was confirmed about when I turned sixteen. During a meeting with a family therapist, my father admitted he was afraid I'd never find love because of my weight. He meant well, but it was a pretty extreme statement. That day my father became a proud spokesperson for the entire male gender, pronouncing on my worth as a woman. On my potential to be desirable.

I failed the test. It was very clear that he thought I was ugly. That even he would never choose me.

Then at around eighteen or nineteen, I tried every possible thing to lose weight. I went from one method to another. Losing weight was my personal mission. It was my whole life. It took up every space.

I lost a little at first, then more and more each year. And that was a relief for everyone. People complimented me. And my parents were proud of me. For the first time, I was told that I was beautiful.

And I understood.

I understood that to be thin was to achieve something important. Something essential.

That being beautiful was the basis of everything.

7

Back at home, I start making a ton of cupcakes for Alice's party.

It's a family tradition. I promised to take care of dessert. Yup, I did.

At least I use a recipe from my own book, *Radiant.* And it makes for great stories.

While my little treasures are in the oven, I look for the perfect outfit. It's quite a challenge to find a look that works with the vibe of her academic friends but still looks like me.

I try on about two thousand combinations and finally choose a gray knit dress with ankle boots.

I'm taking my cupcakes out of the oven when I get a message from Sam.

S: Yeah . . . so turns out I won't be able to go to Alice's. Have to spend the evening at the studio. We're running behind. Need to rearrange October before the tour and it's taking longer than we thought.

Classic Sam. Bailing at the last minute.

E: What? But it'll be boring without you!

S: So don't go ;)

E: It's my sister's birthday and I made 36 cupcakes.

S: Have a good time.

Geez. He could at least have been honest enough to tell me from the beginning that he had no intention of coming, instead of pretending to be interested.

I'll have to go alone, even though I have zero desire to do so.

I receive a new notification. Glimmer of hope.

No, it's Jean-Félix from the agency.

JF: Hello Ellie. Confirming appointment with Mila Mongeau tomorrow 1 p.m. at the office. Hugs.

Nope. Things are really not going my way tonight.

Before leaving, I pass by the mirror. I examine my profile, straighten my shoulders, suck in my stomach. The dress looks good, but maybe a bit too tight?

I take a selfie. If I have 5,000 Likes before 7:00 p.m., I'll wear it. Otherwise, I'll go in jeans.

5 963 Likes

ellie_quinoa_forever Little Saturday night look. Autumn happened or what? **#ootd #fall**

See all 206 comments

vero2016 Always so beautiful

bella_lifestyle Wow great look!

myl_boul take a photo of you and your boyfriend!

ishaisha You are always way too beautiful ❤

nala_lala I would like to see your morning routine. I need a little motivation boost.

fabiola_fleur So lucky to go out with Samuel Vanasse!!!

simone_signo looks like you ate too many of your vegan brownies

martinebeaubien You are magnificent. THANK YOU for inspiring us all. **#TeamEllie**

etienne_black Hi you!

sweet_imagine Looking so very nice

e11evengreys The most beautiful ♥ I would so much like to be like you. I love you.

nancy_doupsy You are SO perfect **#TeamEllie**

le_lepage Yup, some are luckier than others **@sam_van**

bear.ltd Ellie, I lost 20 pounds, but I gained them all back! Do you have any advice for me???

xoxoxoxoxo.me UR too beautiful!! How do you do it?

vivi_guerin You are super beautiful. Where did the dress come from?

lidia.daf You breathe happiness ♥ **#TeamEllie**

Mia__22 Wow très magnifique ♥ ♥ ♥

bussiere9670 Omgggg **#fakesmilealert**

juliette_b @simone_signo re your crap comment . . . dont you have anything else to do with your evening? **#getalife**

elyzabeth_lily Wow

simone_signo @juliette_b Chill! I do what I want with my evenings.

leila_xo but look at how beautiful she is **@ raph.jacob**

karineka HAHAHA **@simone_signo** it's true she's eaten too many gluten-free brownies

math_mathieu12 Gorgeous **@ellie_quinoa_forever**

Suerodrigo Too bad there is no "I love it" button because I would have hit it.

fleurétoilecoeur Ah, look at her, can't take it!

8

7:30 p.m. I open the apartment door and Alice jumps up to greet me. She's been partying for several hours already. The music is loud. We almost have to shout to understand each other.

"Ellie!"

"Happy birthday, baby sister! Twenty-three years!!!"

She gives me a big hug, then takes my jean jacket and throws it on a coat rack already overflowing with scarves and bags of all kinds.

It lands in a puddle of coats on the floor. Alice doesn't even seem to notice.

"Hey, come on in," she says. "I'll introduce you to someone...OMFG cupcakes! Are those the amazing ones with the caramel?"

"No. Squash and flax. With crushed fruit instead of sugar and coconut oil instead of butter. They're super healthy, and you can't even tell."

Alice bursts out laughing. We take a detour through the kitchen where she throws my Tupperware full of cupcakes on the counter with the bowls of chips and plastic cups.

Then she leads me through the strange crowd that populates her living room.

On the couch, three girls are knitting and drinking huge beers. They're relaxed and chatting. Meanwhile, another small group is arguing over a tricky move in Twister.

Alice takes me to her room. On her bed, a guy — fortyish with a small mustache, wool sweater and well-pressed shirt collar — is talking to two girls Alice's age. They seem completely absorbed in whatever it is he's saying.

Alice interrupts them.

"Jeff, this is my sister Ellie. Ellie, this is Jeff. We met at university. He's a soc prof."

I don't even have time to say hello before Alice jumps on the bed to give him a huge kiss. The other two girls look a little uncomfortable.

"I'm Maya, hi," says the taller one. "This is Opale. We take classes with Alice."

"Oh, right, you're her new roommates. I'm Ellie, her sister. Nice to officially meet you."

And out of nowhere, Opale screeches, "Loooool! You're the girl who used to be fat and now goes out with Samuel Vanasse!"

"Uh. Among other things. Yes."

"No offense or anything, but I have absolutely no

respect for what you do."

"Oh. Well, okay, that's your choice."

"Promoting orthorexia and fat shaming — as a feminist I absolutely can't condone it."

"But I'm only trying to help girls who —"

"Lol, no. You're actually just a product of patriarchal oppression. I say all this with respect."

Alice breaks away from Jeff to interrupt.

"Shut up, Opale. Leave my sister alone."

Alice takes my hand and leads me down the long corridor to the kitchen.

"Sorry. She's just a kid, but she's okay."

"No problem, but what is a product of patri —"

"I'll tell you another time. You deserve a beer."

"But do you agree with her?"

"Another time, Ellie. We're here to celebrate. Partay!"

"And that guy Jeff? He's your boyfriend?"

"You know I don't believe in couples."

"I brought kombucha."

"Beer, I said!"

"You're the boss."

∞

I sip my beer alternately with my kombucha while Alice chats with some guys about her program. I listen to them, vaguely wondering what I'm doing here.

It's not that I'm not interested. It's that I get the impression they're just talking to prove they can use three words of more than ten letters in a single sentence. It's heavy going.

At least Alice is all fired up, and that is always quite entertaining.

"Arnaud, stop it! You can't blame anti-male ideology for your obvious lack of sexual magnetism. It's not our fault that you never learned how to spread your seed properly."

I must admit having such a badass sister makes me pretty proud.

I check my cell to see if Sam might have miraculously changed his mind, but no. No news.

∞

8:30 p.m. Another thirty minutes and I'll be able to leave without making Alice mad.

I look at my cupcakes on the counter. Thirty-three of the thirty-six cupcakes are still sitting there. The three that are missing are lying half-eaten on the table.

What a waste.

I take one. Jeff, my sister's Not Boyfriend, shows up in the kitchen. Our eyes meet. He looks me up and down before giving me a kind of sexy wink.

It creeps me out. I give him a little wave anyway, which he seems to find very amusing.

Not me. I feel like a piece of meat. Like the goat in the first Jurassic Park movie.

He dives into the freezer and pulls out four boxes of McCain's cake.

"Deep'n Delicious, folks. It's on me!"

General enthusiasm. Alice brings out forks and everyone happily digs into the small chocolate icing stars. Maya, one of the roommates, gives Alice a bag of little purple pills. She takes one, swallows it with a big sip of IPA and passes the bag to my neighbor. She doesn't even bother handing it to me. I guess she knows it's really not my cup of tea.

∞

9:00 p.m. Everyone is stoned. Everyone except me. Alice goes to the bathroom. This is my cue to quickly slip away.

I'm trying to spot my jean jacket under the gigantic pile of coats in the hall. I've been on all fours for three endless minutes digging around the wool coats and puffy jackets when a tall bearded man throws his coat at me.

It's the last straw.

"Hey!" I scream at him. "Dude, what do you think you're doing?"

"Sorry! I didn't see you." He reaches out one of his big hairy hands to help me up. "Are you a friend of Alice?"

"Her sister."

"Oh, her sister. Wow, you two are so different. I'm David. Dave."

"Ellie."

"You were leaving?"

"Yeah, I…"

"Can I offer you one last beer?"

"No, I…"

"Come on, you can't leave me all alone with them."

Dave points to the gang giving each other a group massage while listening to Coolio in the living room.

His smile is contagious. He seems nice. I burst out laughing.

"I admit that would be cruel. Deal. But just one!"

I follow Dave into the kitchen. Bad idea. I don't know him, I have nothing to say to him. I really should learn to say no, I'll make a vlog about that soon.

I try to quickly think of one last topic of conversation. The weather? Hockey? Bad.

Dave opens a beer, super relaxed.

"So? How's life going for you?"

I answer without even thinking.

"It's going well, thank you. And you?"

Dave looks kind of puzzled.

"No, I mean for real."

"For real, real? Whoa. Big question!"

"Well, we'll probably never see each other again. So, y'know, why not be honest?"

I don't know if it's the beer or fatigue or the day I've had or everything mixed together, but I decide to tell the truth.

"Okay. I'd say it's average."

"Ah, I can sense it. Are you game to tell me why?"

"Good question, but . . . okay. I worry about what people think of me. All the time. And then I think I'm never doing enough. That I'm just not good enough. And it's tough because . . . I never really feel good. Do you ever feel that way?"

"That's it! I love your honesty. Thank you."

"Your turn now."

"Me? I ... I'm okay. I think I've got in this pattern where I like girls who don't like me back, because when girls like me, I don't like them. And even more important, I think I'm doing it on purpose so I'll keep screwing up because I'm afraid of being with anyone because I'm still not over my ex."

"Wow. Deep stuff. I wasn't expecting that."

I'm trying to think of something nice to say when Arnaud, the guy Alice blew off earlier, launches himself at us. He's holding out a cushion and licking his lips like they're candy.

"Okay, guys, is it just me, or is this cushion FUCKING soft?"

David puts on this thoughtful look and pats the cushion.

"No. I can confirm that this is standard softness," he says, dead serious. "What do you think, Ellie?"

I squeeze the pillow.

"Yes, I would say standard softness. For a cushion."

Dave holds a finger in front of his mouth.

"For a cushion. As it were."

We smile at each other. David takes Arnaud by the shoulders.

"Say, have you checked out the living-room sofa? Super soft. It'll blow you away, man."

Arnaud turns back towards the living room with his cushion.

Dave gives me a satisfied look

"Are there pretzels around here somewhere?"

"No, but there are some excellent squash and flax cupcakes."

Dave looks suspiciously at the still-full Tupperware.

"Meh...I'm more Team Pretzels and Chips. Party mix if need be. Bring 'em on."

"By the way, to be authentic to the original German, it's brezel. With a B. Not pretzel."

Dave looks at me, amused. "I didn't mean to offend your German sensibilities."

"I don't want to go on about it, but I did *almost* win a prize in high-school German. It's a fact."

"Wow. Okay, this is a girl who is actually bragging about *almost* winning a prize in high school."

"I am not bragging, BUT I do think it gives me a certain amount of authority on the subject of German snack foods."

"Oh my God."

And we burst out laughing.

∞

Three beers later, I check the time on my cell. 11:30 p.m.

I empty my glass and then I gather up all my mental strength.

"Well..." I say to Dave.

"You're leaving."

"Yeah, I've got a big run tomorrow morning."

"As you wish. But it won't be the same without you."

"It was nice meeting you. Really."

I hesitate. I give him a peck on each cheek. A handshake would be...weird. A hug would be too much.

Crossing the living room, I run into Jeff, the Not Boyfriend, on the dance floor. He's kissing Maya on one side and squeezing Opale's butt on the other.

My sister, on the other hand, is making out with Arnaud on the sofa while keeping one eye on Jeff.

Poor Alice. She really has a gift for getting herself in complicated situations. It must twist her up to see

Jeff kissing her friends at her own party.

I hope she's going to be okay. I'll call her tomorrow.

I go back to digging through the pile of coats and finally find my jacket. I have my hand on the doorknob when Dave joins me in the hall. He has a cushion in his hands.

"Just to confirm, this cushion here. Standard softness, right?"

I smile and reach out to squeeze the cushion. I pretend to think about it.

"Affirmative."

There's silence.

"Okay, then. Bye."

"Bye."

We just stand there. And it hits me. Dave has gorgeous eyes. Eyes that are fixed right on me. In his gaze there's a mix of gentleness and strength that just...I'm...I hesitate.

Okay, this is awkward. I lean forward to get rid of the weird feeling.

I'll give him two quick pecks and go.

I'm almost at his cheek when I remember that I already did this before. Too late to pull back. I'll have to go through with it now, but I have a moment of doubt. I'm aiming for the wrong side. Or is it Dave that's getting it wrong?

In any case, our mouths meet.

When I realize we're kissing, I push Dave away. He stumbles back, trips on a bag, falls onto the coats.

Shit.

"Sorry!" I say.

And I hurry away down the stairs.

FAKE

Judging influencers is a guilty little pleasure for quite a few people. Me, for one. I did it a lot before becoming one myself. I wrote what my haters write about me most often (well, apart from the fact that I'm "not that pretty") — that influencers are fake.

I used to get riled up when people thought that. I would always answer them. I tried to win their love with emojis and going all I-respect-your-opinion.

Now...it's different. I'd never admit this publicly, but I wonder whether they have a point. I mean, we always talk about how important it is to be authentic, but is it even possible to not be fake on social media? Would people still want to follow me if I was completely myself?

Maybe we get more fake over time.

When you first start to be successful on social media, everything is new, everything is fun. You give 2000 percent. And you set certain standards for yourself.

At first, I never missed a workout, I followed my meal plan religiously, I posted photos every day, I offered lots of new recipes, I always had a new outfit, I answered all my messages...

It gets exhausting over time, being that person. You end up taking shortcuts.

I'm not deliberately lying to my followers, you understand. It's just that there's a small gap between the girl that I am and the one that I would like to become. I can't deny that the internet allows me to look like the girl I would like to be more often than who I really am. Does that necessarily make me a fake?

You know, when I look back at my old posts, for example, I realize that I often stick in a #happiness. But the truth is that I hardly ever feel like that. I hardly ever feel good. Even today I'm trying hard, but I'm not quite getting there, to happiness. When I hit a goal, I'm happy for about thirty seconds. Then there are five more that appear in my head.

It's like succeeding isn't as rewarding as I thought it would be at the beginning. I still need something else to feel good.

Isn't it like that for you?

9

The sound of my alarm clock hits me like a shovel in the face. For a girl with a morning workout, I went to bed way too late last night. I almost crashed into bed fully dressed when I got home, but I forced myself to take a shower and brush my teeth. A heroic gesture I'm grateful for now.

To-do list for the day: Replace snacks with green smoothies to make up for all the beer I drank. Hit the road jogging at a pace of at least five and a half minutes a kilometer, and do five sets of crunches. Buy an organic chicken breast. Work meeting with Mila Mongeau. Which I should just cancel and postpone until...forever.

No, but it's true that instead of wasting my time with Mila, I could be planning my posts for the next month. Figure out a way to improve my stats. Prepare amazing videos. Finish moving in. And text Alice to find out if she's okay.

OH DAMN IT.

Dave.

I forgot all about Dave.

Kissing someone not on purpose is okay, right?

Clearly not my fault. Clearly not my kind of guy anyway.

I'm just going to put this behind me and never think about it again. It was just a stupid...mouth accident.

I flinch when Sam rolls over to hug me, his big arm still warm from being under the covers all night.

"I didn't hear you come in. Have a good time with the brainiacs?"

"Mmhmmm. Right..."

"Wait!" With a single superhuman leap, Sam jumps out of bed and starts rummaging around in the gigantic pile of clothes I left on the floor while I was trying on outfits for Alice's party.

"Don't move."

"What? What is it?"

"..."

"Sam, tell me!"

"Hang on...just...don't move!"

I watch Sam rummaging through my things. It's not really rational, but I start to panic a little. I see Dave again. His mouth. The expression on his face when he fell into the coats.

Calm down. There's no possible way that Sam

could know. If he did, he wouldn't be digging around in my laundry.

But why is he holding my jean jacket in his hands?

Worse comes to worst, I'll just explain what happened. He can't leave me over this. No, it's impossible.

I take a deep breath for courage when Sam finally finds what he's looking for in the pile of dirty laundry.

His phone, which he left in his jeans pocket.

Holding it up triumphantly, he says, "I have a video idea for your channel."

"Oh, cool," I say, trying to look completely normal. "What is it?"

I'm half listening to his answer.

"We'll film our morning routine. Just do what you always do."

Sam jumps on the bed and starts filming. He kisses me on the cheek.

"Good morning, my love."

I come to my senses and slam the iPhone into the duvet.

"Not now! I have to do my run."

"Act like nothing's happening. Just get ready for your run. I'll take care of everything. It'll be great."

Sam tries to put his phone back in front of my face, but I stop him.

"Well, wait! I have to get myself ready before —"

"Ellie, your followers aren't a bunch of chumps. They'll be able to tell you're wearing makeup and know this isn't real."

"Yes…but…no, I…"

"Just trust me. Anyway, if there's anything you don't like, I'll fix it in the edit. Close your eyes."

"…"

"Close your eyes!"

"Arrgh! Okay, okay."

Sam pulls the covers over my shoulders and starts the video again. I find it weird, but to make him happy, I pretend to wake up. I even blow a little kiss to the camera just to fool around.

"Good morning, my beauty."

"Morning, tiger."

We spend a good hour filming our routine. Sam tickling me in bed, me brushing my teeth with my mouth full of toothpaste, Sam shaving, making faces, me making a smoothie, the two of us kissing on the couch.

I admit it's fun. I will never post this — the quality

isn't good enough — but it's still fun to spend time with Sam. And we can show this to our kids one day.

OMG, I can't believe I just thought that.

When we're done and I'm ready, I put on my sneakers and head off for my run.

Behind me, I hear Sam shouting, "Yeah, it's gonna be da bomb!"

#HEALTHYLIVING

Drink water. Zero percent Greek yogurt. Put down your fork. Reduce your portions. Learn to love yourself. Do ten sit-ups before bed. Kale. No eating after 7:00 p.m. Weigh yourself every morning. Find your Why. Take up a sport. Count calories. Probiotics. Skip breakfast. The power of celery. Drink more water. Stay away from the basket of bread. Follow an eating plan. Avoid liquid calories. Ask for the vinaigrette on the side. Stay strong. Cut out sugar. Choose yourself first. Go on a detox. Take a bath. Hot lemon water when you wake up. Avoid fat. Go veggie. Green tea. Consider that breakfast is the most important meal of the day. Take natural supplements. Get more sleep. Exercise more. Ban carbs. Egg white omelets. Plan. Take the stairs. Cook. Eat more, but better. Bet on protein. Avoid ripe bananas. Stay on the program. Don't give up. Just have one bite. Herbal tea. No pasta, no bread, no potatoes. Drink cider vinegar. Exercise, exercise, exercise. Love yourself enough. Fast. Choose the salad. Don't diet. Keep a food journal. Organize your refrigerator. Guilt makes you fat. Breathe. Spit it out. Do better tomorrow. Get off the bus one stop early and walk. Portions no bigger than the palm of your hand. Prebiotics. Connect with nature. Eat six small meals a day. Track your calories. Engage your muscles while you work out. Above all, do not deprive yourself of the essential nutrients in egg yolks. Do your meal prep. CrossFit. Smoothies. Eat intuitively. Select your restaurant meal in advance. Visualize. Boost your metabolism. Brush your teeth instead of having a snack. Baby carrots. Chew gum. Eat only between noon and 8:00 p.m. Run. Avoid processed food. Always have a post-workout snack. Recognize the signs. Weigh your food. Don't go grocery shopping on an empty stomach. Consume good fats. Adopt a healthy lifestyle. Start fresh on Mondays. Don't step on the scale too often. Chew each mouthful at least twenty times. Grapefruit. Eat less. Take action. No matter what happens, do not give in. Eat fiber. Count steps. RESIST. Go for a walk. Love yourself more, love yourself for real. Drink water.

Text messages between Ellie and Alice

E: Hi! How are you? Just to let you know I'm here if you wanna talk.

A: That's okay.

E: Cool. Sure you don't want to talk about . . .

A: ?

E: About Jeff and your other friends . . . yesterday at the party . . .

E: You know what I mean.

A: No.

E: No what? You know, right? That they were making out . . .

A: Ellie, stop. It's annoying.

E: Huh? Just asking if you're OK?

10

I'm making a protein smoothie. Sitting at the kitchen island, Sam is editing our morning routine video. From time to time he makes little sounds like "Hmm," "Nah," "Yup."

I've already had to remind him twice not to waste his time on that, but he says it's just for fun. Good.

As for me, I still haven't had the guts to cancel my meeting with Mila Mongeau. I have fifty minutes to get to the agency. I have a queasy stomach and my hands are sweating.

I just don't want to go. I want to forget it exists. I would take twelve hours of back-to-back yoga sessions with my mother over a single minute with Mila Mongeau.

I interrupt my food preparation.

"I'm not going," I announce. "I'm going to say I'm sick."

"No, no. You can't pass up this opportunity."

"But I HATE her, Mila Mongeau."

"It's been, what, ten years since you saw her? I'll bet she's changed. Look at her Insta. You clearly want this girl on your team. She looks great."

I can't help myself.

"She looks great? You mean she's super attractive."

"I didn't say that."

I watch him out of the corner of my eye. I don't believe it.

I take an apple and a kiwi from the fruit bowl.

"Seriously, can you explain to me what a girl who has a DIY and deco channel is doing CONSTANTLY posting half-naked pictures of herself? It's so boring."

"She has a beautiful body and she shows it off. I don't see what the problem is."

I grab a knife, slice the fruit in quarters and throw them in the blender with a handful of spinach. I add two big spoonfuls of vanilla protein powder.

I don't want to continue this discussion about Mila, but Sam insists.

"You can't deny that her photos are very beautiful."

"You mean her butt."

"No, her photos! They have an unusual visual quality. I'm not kidding. You should do the same thing. It's an excellent strategy. And proof that it works is that we're talking about it."

"Sam! I have followers who are thirteen years old. I'm not going to start posting photos of myself in a thong. I have a certain responsibility to —"

Okay. It's true. But to be completely honest, if I don't post photos like Mila, it's because I have this hangup about my stomach. It's still a bit soft below my bellybutton. Like a deflated balloon. It bulges a bit. The fat is gone, but the extra skin is still there. It's not very Insta friendly.

I start the blender. I watch the fruit swirl around. Sam stays planted in front of me. He waits for the motor to stop.

"Not only that, but if you don't go to your meeting, what kind of message do you think that sends to Malik? That you're not serious. That you're not ready to do the work."

"But I am serious! Look, I work super hard."

"I don't doubt that, Ellie, but you've also been really lucky. There are a lot of YouTubers out there, and if I were in Malik's shoes, I might really think that you're not the kind of girl who's determined to —"

I put my hand in front of his mouth to make him stop talking.

Sometimes I wonder if Sam isn't jealous of my success on social media. As if being a famous musician gives him a legitimacy that I don't have. As if

he secretly thinks that he deserves to have more followers than me.

"It's all good. You win. I'll go."

"No, Ellie. You're the one who wins. Don't forget,
it's your business, it's your —"

"Just...shush."

Sam grabs me around the waist and pinches my
bum. He kisses me.

"It's a good thing you're so good-looking, because
you're a real asshole," I say.

"By the way, have you seen my peanut butter
cookies? They've been missing since yesterday."

"Haven't seen them. Clearly you already ate them."

I give him a big kiss on the cheek.

Do you ever imagine yourself doing really weird things?

For the past month or two, it's been happening to me a lot. In the heat of the moment, I think about doing or saying something that could be disastrous.

Like smashing my gum into someone's hair. Screaming during a moment of quiet. Pouring my latte in my mother's purse. Telling the truth when someone asks what I'm thinking. Kissing a perfect stranger.

For a split second, things like this cross my mind. It's not that I want to do them. On the contrary. I'm terrified of the possibility that I might.

I read once that vertigo isn't so much the fear of heights as it is the fear of jumping. The fear of being seized with an uncontrollable impulse and just…doing it.

Do you know what I'm talking about? Like sometimes when I hold a knife, I imagine sticking it in my hand. I try to reassure myself. To tell myself that there is absolutely no chance that I will actually do it…but I only half believe that.

Because it's already happened to me — getting a bad idea and then going with it.

It was two days before the graduate exhibition at the end of high school.

And I have only myself to blame.

11

I'm waiting for Mila Mongeau in one of the big conference rooms at the agency. I nervously tap the lid of the mason jar holding my smoothie. Believe me — seeing your worst enemy from high school is a real appetite killer.

Jean-Félix bursts into the room. He's out of breath.

"She's here! Mila! She was...stuck in the subway breakdown. Between Joliette and Préfontaine. Can you imagine? Between two stations!"

Mila walks into the conference room. Under her big scarf, she looks completely deflated. I force myself to smile. It's important that she doesn't think it's a big deal for me to see her again.

"Worst day ever. I imagine you're in a rush, too."

"Yeah...actually, not really...well, a little."

Shit, shit, shit. I am really bad at looking relaxed.

"Okay, listen, it's simple. I know we'll be never friends. And that's okay. YouTube friendships never end well. We can pretend for four videos and a few posts. If it works, great. If not, we'll stop and everyone's good. Okay with you?"

"Y-yes..."

Mila talks so fast, I don't have time to ask myself whether it's okay with me or not. My only goal is to appear to be in control of the situation.

The keywords here are "appear to be," because in fact I have zero control.

"Okay, let's make a video on fall decor trends," Mila continues. "A Q&A, a recipe, then for the fourth, you can do a workout or stretch routine, whatever you want, I don't care."

"Okay!"

"We'll release two on my channel, then two on yours, but I'd like it to be on your IGTV, too. We'll have to film a vertical version just for that. And we film everything at the same time. It'll be easier. In the meantime, I'll prepare a story to promote the launch of your book. If you can integrate one of my scented candles in an Instagram post, we have a deal."

"Deal."

"Take this one, I've got plenty." Mila slides a small gold cardboard box in front of me. It says *Ambiance x Mila.*

I open it. It smells like vanilla and cinnamon.

"Is Monday good for shooting the clips? I'll send you a google doc with the schedule."

"Yes. Perfect."

"Um, so, Ellie..."

"What?"

"It's cool, what you've made of yourself. I'm happy for you."

This takes me completely by surprise.

"Thanks. You, too. And your illustrations are beautiful. Your other things, too, but it's your illustrations that I like best."

Mila looks at me, surprised. She looks at me like I'm a Martian.

"Thank you," she says.

"..."

"I didn't tell Malik that we knew each other because I don't want him to think we're friends. We're collaborating as professionals. Not because we went to high school together."

"Absolutely."

"Cool. At least we're clear on that." Mila nods, satisfied. Then she gathers up her bag and disappears down the hall.

THROWBACK

Things got complicated with Mila just before the graduating exhibition in our final year. We were each working on a personal project in art class.

I was struggling to create a clay sculpture that was supposed to represent the existential void. Mila was working on a gigantic canvas. For her, it was more than an end-of-year project. It had become her whole life. A way of compensating for having to leave the volleyball team, maybe.

One morning when I was late for first period, I found a large container of spring mix lettuce in front of my locker. I didn't know what it was doing there, but I didn't have time to think about it. I kicked it aside, grabbed my books and ran to my lab.

The next day at noon, I found another container in front of my locker, but this time there was a note written on it with marker: *For Élisabeth. I'm sick of seeing your fat ass in school. Time you started eating salad. MUCHO LOVE. Everybody.*

I felt like I'd been slapped in the face.

It was so . . . mean. I hadn't done anything to deserve this.

Okay, so I wasn't "thin," but wasn't that my problem? I found it cruel that someone wanted to rub it in. As if it wasn't already hard enough.

I didn't sleep for days. I was afraid it would start up again. I wondered how many people were involved. If there were secret groups on the internet set up just to laugh at me....

I became completely paranoid.

It took some time, but I ended up finding out who had done it.

Text messages between Alice and Ellie

A: Ellie, we have to see each other, IT'S URGENT.

E: Are you okay? Where are you??

A: Café B corner Laurier and St-André.

E: I could be there in 30 minutes.

A: OK. Waiting for you.

12

I rush to the cafe at breakneck speed. I'm so happy Alice is finally opening up about her ridiculous love life. She was acting like she was above all that stuff, but I don't believe it. If I were in her place, I'd be devastated if my date was kissing one or more of my friends at my birthday. This is a normal human reaction.

In short, I'm happy to be able to support Alice through this heartbreak. As per our tradition, I've even brought her a bar of chocolate.

All our traditions are sweet ones. It's always been that way.

When Alice sees me, she closes *The Wreck of Civilizations*, carefully slipping in a napkin so as not to lose her place.

As usual, I do a quick scan. Bulky knit sweater, fountain ponytail, lips dry as sandpaper. I'd say feeling a bit nauseous with a two-out-of-five migraine.

She gives me a big hug.

"Thanks for coming, Ellie! You've saved my life."

"No problem, muffin. It can't be fun, what you're going through."

"You know about it? It's so unfair. I never thought

she would go this far."

For a second I'm not sure I understand what she's talking about. Her?

Maya! Right, through this whole saga I've been so thoroughly focused on Jeff that I completely lost sight of the fact that she was also betrayed by her friend Maya.

Poor Alice.

"No kidding," I say. "A girl who goes around kissing your Not Boyfriend is no friend."

"What are you talking about?" Alice looks at me, puzzled. "Ellie, I'm talking about Maman! She doesn't want to pay for my sociology degree. I have five days to find the money for this semester or I'm out of the program."

"Ah, right!"

"It would be nothing for her to pay for my course and cover part of my rent. If I'd decided to do an MBA, you can bet she'd have been happy to pull out her checkbook. But sociology is apparently a "waste of my potential.""

I can't believe this.

"Can't you get a loan or grant?"

"Just loans because our parents are too rich. But

I don't see why I should go into debt when the money is just sitting in Maman's retirement fund."

"Okay. So what are you going to do?"

"I have an idea. That's what I wanted to talk to you about."

I've been outmaneuvered like a rank beginner. This is Alice the Great at her finest. Getting me to rush over at top speed laden with sweets and sympathy just to participate in her shenanigans.

Alice starts explaining her plan.

"You hardly have to do a thing," Alice explains. "Just organize a dinner with Papa."

"Papa! First of all, no. Second, if Maman doesn't want to give you money, you can be sure that he will have been expressly forbidden from doing so, too. There's no way, Alice."

"Yeah, I thought about that. I'm sure I can win him over. As long as I can button him up first. That's why he needs to think it's your idea to have dinner."

"It's butter him up, Alice. Not button."

I'm still completely confused when the server arrives to take my order. It takes about two seconds for me to recognize Opale, one of Alice's roommates. More precisely the one who, and I quote, "has no respect for what I do." I find her much more pleasant as a server than when she looked straight down on me from Alice's queen bed.

I'm guessing she has no choice but to be nice to customers. Either way, it's a refreshing change.

"I'll have a matcha latte with soy milk in a bowl."

"Uh, we don't have that. Sorry."

"Don't have what?"

"No matcha, no soy, and we don't do bowls."

While Opale's contemptuous gaze makes a big comeback, I gather what's left of my goodwill.

"Almond milk chai?" I ask.

"Don't have that, either. We have green tea or chamomile. And oat milk. The intensive cultivation of soybeans and almonds has already wreaked enough havoc."

"Well, just green tea in a cup, thank you."

There is officially no hope for Opale and me. She leaves us. I roll my eyes. Alice is texting away on her phone.

"Charming," I say.

"Yes. I spend my life here. It's really cool. I have a lot of friends who work as baristas. So, okay, first step, call Papa and tell him you want to introduce him to

Sam, your new boyfriend."

Alice begins to explain her plan to me in detail, but I cut her off pretty fast. I don't want to know.

"Forget it, Alice. I won't do it."

She heaves a big sigh. I lean back in my chair.

A big hairy hand puts a mini teapot in front of me. Relieved to be rid of the bitchy Opale, I look up at my savior.

"Hey, Dave!" My sister throws herself in his arms to give him a hug.

I stay in my seat, paralyzed.

I never thought for one second that I would see him again. Let alone here. Today.

Things go downhill from there. In a burst of enthusiasm, Alice makes the introductions.

"Dave, my sister. My sister, Dave."

"Nice to meet you," I say.

"We know each other," Dave says.

Damn it. What was I thinking, pretending we've never met? WTF!

I try to recover with the first thing that comes into my mind.

"Yes, I remember. We talked at the party, didn't we?"

Alice, who apparently knows nothing about us

meeting at her party, says, "Must have been a memorable conversation."

I laugh nervously. I'm still trying to think of something to say when Dave walks away, throwing me a look that's half incredulous and half amused.

"I'm drooling to the power of a thousand," Alice says. "If it were up to me I'd have tried to snag him long ago. Maya and Opale have also tried, but no luck. He doesn't believe in one-night stands. Also, apparently he has a really big one. What a waste. Anyway. Seriously, if I can't find the money before…"

Alice keeps talking, but I have stopped listening. I watch Dave pour an espresso before disappearing into the kitchen.

It's true that he is good-looking in his own way.

"Ellie, really, if I call Papa he'll guess that I want to ask him for money. Please, I'll owe you one. You can ask me for anything you want."

"Okay."

"YES! I knew you'd say yes. You're the best. I have to go. I have a meeting for my group project at five."

"You really are the worst, Alice Bourdon-Marois. You'd better pay for my green tea and then be grateful for all eternity."

PAPA

Last year of junior high. First term. I bring home my report card. I put it in a Duo-Tang to keep it beautiful.

My father is sitting at his desk. Silently I pull out the long blue-and-white sheet from my huge backpack. From my *Titanic*-sized backpack. I hand him the precious piece of paper.

I have good marks. Not like my usual. It'll be a surprise. I tell him I got my report. But I don't smile. I want him to be amazed. Stunned.

I watch him read it. He takes his time. I'm scared. I'm still scared of my father. He can get worked up. Be demanding.

But this time, I'm not worried. My grades in math and written French are excellent. In written French, I usually make too many mistakes. But not this time. This time, I've done a good job.

My father says he's happy. That's good. He's worried about me getting into the private school he's chosen, but he's made arrangements with the director. A friend of a friend. He has contacts. I would be admitted as long as my grades improve in first semester. And they have.

I'm proud. I've achieved something. Something important.

"I guess we can't fix everything at the same time — your grades and your weight," he adds.

I freeze. My weight. I'm fat. I can't win.

"No, you're right," I say, barely whispering. "I was concentrating on my marks."

"I understand," my father replies gently. "One thing at a time."

"Yes … one thing at a time."

I failed. I'm sinking.

My father. I can't win.

13

Alice starts to collect her things and gets ready to leave. I'm looking for my cell. My eyes fall on the screen already lit up on the phone deep in my bag. I have at least a million notifications and they keep coming in.

My heart is trampolining. My fingers tremble as I try to find out where they're coming from.

YouTube

Flavie_racine commented: LOL LOL LOL . . .

Juliesusu has sent you a message

Mylène_chat commented: You are officially . . .

Zozoé98 commented: Woot you're too . . .

Sté_2001 commented: Sam is too handsome . . .

MilèneMi commented: I like your curtains

EmmaB commented: Laughed my head . . .

Gina B has sent you a message

Cottoncandy99 has sent you a message

I open my YouTube app. I can hardly believe my eyes.

Sam posted our morning routine video on my channel without showing it to me.

Impossible. He must have made a mistake. I call him in a panic.

He picks up after two rings.

"I told you it would be da bomb!"

"Are you kidding me? You posted the video?! I haven't even seen it yet!"

"Fifty thousand views in an hour. ONE hour! Oh, shit, 50,100."

"..."

"It's going viral. The fans are going crazy — 50,500 views!"

I hang up. I grab my headphones to watch the video. Alice blows me a kiss before disappearing from my field of vision.

My belly does backflips as I press Play.

Sam has made a super catchy montage to a pop song played on the ukulele. You can see me waking up with no makeup on, eating in my underwear, kissing Sam. I say lots of ridiculous stuff.

I wasn't doing this seriously. I was 99.9 percent

sure it would never be published.

Shit, shit, shit. I will become a running joke. I'm terrified at the thought of reading the comments.

They're going to slaughter me.

I scroll through the messages under the video.

Lula Bye 5 minutes ago
You are officially my idol and the funniest person in the world!!! Your video is just too dreamy wow **#couplegoals**

Plume rose 10 minutes ago
Hahahaha a smooooziiiie! I WANT THE RECIPE. You are the best couple ever. **#jealousy**

JoannieBé 15 minutes ago
SO BEAUTIFUL OMG I'M DYING.

Simone Vu 15 minutes ago
But when are we going to see Sam naked? Marry me Sam!!!!!!!!!!!!!!!

Croquette Coquette 20 minutes ago
LOL. Looks like you don't have kids! It is completely unrealistic to think that everyone has time to make a smoothie and go for a run in the morning. Get out of your Unicorn World!

Minh Minh 20 minutes ago

Seriously, I want your liiiife. I can't stand how cute you are.
xxx

. . .

Deep breath. People like it. That calms me down a bit, but I still can't believe that 50,500 people saw this before I did.

What right does Sam have to post videos on my channel without telling me?

We'll just see about that!

And I rush out of the cafe in a panic.

14

I step onto the sidewalk, determined to set a few
things straight with Sam, when a voice stops me.

"Excuse me! You can't just walk out without paying!"

I turn around. Dave is standing in the doorway,
all smiles. He has a pencil behind his ear and a dishcloth in his hands.

I go back and I try to explain the situation.

"Uh, look," I stammer. "Sorry...I thought Alice
had paid for me and —"

"Ellie, I'm kidding. It's on the house. I just wanted
to say goodbye."

"Thank you, but you don't have to do that. I wasn't
trying to steal. I'll pay for it."

I dig into my bag for my wallet.

Dave is watching me closely.

"Are you okay?" he asks.

His question catches me off guard. I want to say
yes, but I can't make the word come out of my mouth.

I look down. I look through my bag. I feel hot.

I look at Dave. His eyes are fixed on me. Soft. Kind.

I try to speak, but my mouth refuses to cooperate.

Instead I make fluttery motions with my hands. It's

really embarrassing. I swallow my emotions as best I can.

"I'm good," I end up saying.

But it hardly looks like it and, anyway, I feel tears coming to my eyes.

Dave must have a superpower. It's impossible to hide how I'm feeling from him.

"Actually, not really. I'm not."

Dave smiles at me. His kindness makes me feel good, even if I'm finding the whole situation incredibly embarrassing.

"Sorry, it's a lot. Oh, my God. Sorry...I'm just a bit...dizzy. It'll pass."

"Hey, it's okay. Do you want to walk a little?"

"Yes. Good idea."

"Where are you headed?"

"To the metro...you'd better let your boss know?"

"The boss knows, don't worry."

Dave gives me a little wink. I don't get it.

When I don't react, he adds, "I'm the boss. I was making a little joke."

"Ah, okay. It's your café?"

"Yeah. I bought it three years ago with a small inheritance from my father."

He gently takes me by the shoulders.

"Breathe," he says.

I take a deep breath to calm myself.

"It's a really nice place," I say. "Congratulations."

Dave keeps smiling at me. It makes me blush. I stare at the sidewalk in front of me. We're walking side by side. Our arms brush against each other.

"Although I am somewhat disappointed by your selection of teas."

"Meh. Tea. Not a fan. It's boring, don't you think?"

I pretend to be shocked. This seems to amuse Dave.

"Well, Ellie, you must admit that tea tastes like nothing. Take lemonade or hot chocolate. Now that's taste. But tea basically requires autosuggestion. You need extreme concentration to discern any taste at all. Admit it!"

I laugh and look right in his eyes.

"Excuse me, but you are completely off base. Tea is the beverage of the future. Antioxidants, polyphenols, flavonoids... Hello, future. Hello..."

When my eyes meet his, I'm off balance. I stare at his pupils and it's like I'm afraid I'm going to fall right into them.

I don't think he notices.

Instead, he bursts out laughing, too.

"Flavonoids! Are you serious? No, I don't believe it. Clearly tea is overrated."

His arm brushes against mine.

I like this. I wonder whether he's doing it on purpose. Surely not.

I say the first thing that comes into my head.

"I'll tell you what's overrated."

"Go ahead."

"Paninis."

Dave throws up his hands.

"Absolutely not! They're like the most beautiful invention in the world. Obviously you don't like hot sandwiches. That is truly shocking. Wraps, I would understand. They're wet, they get all mushy, you never know how to hold them."

"Okay. You don't understand. I HATE wraps."

"Finally, a bit of common sense!"

"Have you noticed that the bread part is always some weird color like yellow or orange? Seriously? Who wants to eat orange bread?"

"Nobody!"

"Nobody at all."

We keep talking for another two or five or fifteen minutes. I don't know, I completely lose track of time.

When we arrive at the metro, reality catches up with me. I think about my makeup-less face in Sam's video, the upcoming collaboration with Mila Mongeau, dinner with my father...

I turn to Dave to say goodbye. He sees right away that my mood has changed. He looks into my eyes.

"I don't know what made you feel dizzy, Ellie, but I'd like to help."

Mini internal collapse. I'd like to keep walking to all the stations on the Orange Line with him. Tell him that I feel good when he's around. That I don't want him to leave.

Instead, what comes out of my mouth is, "Thanks, but I'm already feeling better."

"That's great. Fantastic."

"Yeah."

"Good," he says. "So, well, I promise not to try to kiss you this time...Not without a nice pile of coats to fall into. Way too risky."

Dave looks at me. It's like he's waiting for me to react, but nothing happens.

"...for when you push me..." he continues. "That

was an attempt at a joke. Didn't quite pull it off."

He laughs.

"You tried to kiss me?" I ask, dead serious.

Dave looks at me, surprised. He must think I'm losing it.

I try to clarify. "I mean, I thought it was me!"

"You thought you tried to kiss me?"

"No! I thought it was a mouth accident."

"A mouth accident?"

"Well...yeah. That can happen, can't it?"

"No, Ellie. I can confirm that I tried to kiss you."

My heart goes boom. A big boom. I blush to the power of a thousand.

Dave, who, I notice, still has a pencil behind his ear and a dishcloth over his shoulder, looks at me like he's delighted.

"Aaahh. Okay," I stammer. "Thank you."

"Thank you for trying to kiss you?" He's starting to look way too happy watching me fumbling. If he didn't notice my embarrassment before, he sure notices it now.

I have to get a grip.

"No! Thank you for...being...nice and...just forget it, Dave... Dave what?"

"David Lanctôt."

"Okay, great. Super. So, goodbye, David Lanctôt."

"Bye, Ellie."

I move to say goodbye. I hesitate. Handshake? No. Kisses on the cheek? Forget it. There's just one option.

"Hug?"

"Yeah, sure."

Dave hugs me. He smells good. He holds me just tight enough. Just gently enough. I am full up. I silently award him a doctorate in hugging.

It's going on for maybe just the tiniest bit too long, when Dave says, "Okay, Ellie, I am going to pull away to the left, and you pull back to the right. Wouldn't want to cause any kind of mouth accident."

"My God, you're an asshole."

We let go. I give him one last little wave before rushing into the metro. I smile like a fool thinking about our discussion about wraps. I try to remember his smell. I wonder where he lives. What kind of music he listens to. If he thinks I'm pretty. If he finds me interesting.

I remember that we semi kissed at Alice's party. It makes me feel strange.

When I get to the turnstile, I come to my senses.
Dear God, what is happening to me?!

CELEBRITY WORLD

Influencer Jordanne Jacques is dumped by girl-friend on social media

Model and LGBTQ+ activist Marine Lorrain insists that she was the one who broke up with Jordanne Jacques, in an Instagram post recounting the last moments she spent with the young entrepreneur when they traveled to India. This is how we learned that . . .

Ellie of Quinoa Forever and Samuel Vanasse are too HOT in their new video!

#CoupleGoals Alert. While we were still recovering from the wonderful photos of their trip to Costa Rica, the couple, who have just moved in together, posted an adorable video of their morning routine. Once again, the lovebirds surprise us in the most unexpected . . .

A fan says that Cath Bonenfant saved her from suicide

Known for her transparency, the beautiful Cath never hesitates to address sensitive subjects like depression, anorexia and anxiety. By opening up about such taboos, she has become a comforting figure for many people who are going through difficult times. Such as Jade, 18, who . . .

Text messages between Malik and Ellie

M: Élisabeth, your new video is brilliant! We would be very interested to meet with Sam. I have a proposal to make.

M: I'm away for another 72 hours. See you Friday 1:30 p.m.?

E: OK!!

15

I push open the door of the condo at full speed and throw my keys on the floor.

"Sam! You're here?"

He's in the bath. His big arms float in the lavender bubbles.

I know I should still be mad, but I'm just so happy that Malik is happy.

"Malik wants to see us. He has a proposal for us."

"Yeah, that's wild!"

"You're a genius. Thank you, thank you, thank you, thank you." I lean in to kiss him. He grabs me by the waist and pulls me into the tub fully clothed.

There's soapy water everywhere, but I don't care. He kisses me.

"You and me . . . we are unbeatable, Ellie."

I look Sam in the eye. He is so completely, absolutely with me.

I see myself laughing with Dave.

I don't know what got into me. It really is not the way things are right now. I mean, come on. I'm dating Samuel Vanasse. Things have never gone so well for me since we've been together. It would be completely ridiculous to...

I'm just going to stop thinking about Dave immediately and make sure our paths never cross again. Never.

There you go, that's an excellent plan. It's all behind me already.

"Ellie, are you okay?"

"Yes, sorry...I love you, Sam."

"I know."

Text messages between Ellie and Jacques

E: Papa, hi! I'd like to get together for dinner. What about tomorrow? I want to introduce you to my boyfriend. We could invite Alice too! xx

J: Great to hear from you. Tomorrow is good for me. At D'Astous same as last time?

E: Great! I'll reserve a table.

Text messages between Ellie and Alice

E: Papa tomorrow at 7 p.m. at D'Astous.

A: YES. Show time!

16

Mother-daughter yoga. Middle of the front row. The virabhadrasana, Warrior Pose.

I know this one. Nico puts his hand on my back to help me deepen my breath. My mother is watching us out of the corner of her eye. She raises her hand to speak.

"Nico, is my pelvis aligned?"

"I'm coming, Estelle, just a second."

But instead of going to my mother, Nico turns to adjust the foot of the person behind me and says, "Prepare for bakasana, Crane Pose."

He continues to the back of the class, completely ignoring my mother. She tries to get his attention yet again.

"I could use some help, Nicooo." She draws out the O in Nico in an irritating way.

He answers right away. "Try to calm your fifth chakra, Estelle. That should help."

Oh, no. I suddenly get it.

Nico knows that my mother is fantasizing about his young toned body. He realizes that she's using the moments when he touches her to imagine herself curled up in his arms. Being taken, desired, loved. And he's revolted by it.

That's why he's avoiding her this morning.

I look at my mother, pathetic in her too-tight yoga gear. I know she gets it, too. She pretends to be focused on her Crane Pose, but her inner world is silently crumbling. I can see it in her eyes. In her tight smile, her tense arms.

I feel bad for her. I want to put my arms around her, tell her he isn't worth it. That he doesn't know what he's missing.

No chance of that happening. My mother just stares straight ahead, too proud to show what she's feeling.

The class continues without incident. Nico doesn't check on my mother the whole time. I admit it's a relief, a bit of a break from those uncomfortable moments. I can concentrate on my form in peace.

"I invite you to settle in for the final relaxation, savasana, and to reconnect with your opening intention and let it resonate within you."

My mother gets up and walks out of the room, leaving all her things on the floor. I stay, because I know savasana is a sacred time. I mean, it's written in the code of honor that they make you sign at registration. Savasana is a sacred moment. You can't just leave before. Not unless you're willing to commit a highly transgressive act.

When I get to my locker, I get a short message. My mother apologizes for rushing away. An important appointment, she says.

My poor, poor maman.

David Lanctôt has sent you a Facebook message

D: OK, I admit I googled you. I wasn't expecting this. Know that it is an honor for me to be your 112,384th Facebook follower. Come by the café sometime. xx

17

Mila lives in a condo downtown. The kind of condo you've seen six thousand times on the tours of influencer houses on YouTube. She has a clothes rack in her room where she displays her most beautiful outfits, two hundred thousand fluffy cushions and as many green plants as there are shelves on the walls — at least three hundred and fifty.

She looks over her notes for her DIY while drinking from a huge cup with gold letters saying, *Keep calm and be yourself.*

Without raising her eyes from her script, she says, "You understand that I'm going to play this BFF game, but it's just for the videos."

"Yeah, of course."

While she gathers together the things she needs for her affordable autumn look, I take in the large illustrations and watercolors on her living-room walls.

They are wonderful. Mila did them, that's for sure. I'd recognize her style anywhere. A mix of pop and impressionism with splotches of vibrant color.

I've always been a fan. I'm relieved to see that she's kept up with her painting. I want to ask whether she kept the canvas from the year-end exhibition of our last year at high school. I wonder what it would be like to see it again now.

But I'm not up for talking about that with her.

Instead I say, "You could be a real artist. Sell your work, exhibit in galleries...I'd buy it, for sure. Wouldn't you like that?"

"Thanks. Yeah, I think about it sometimes. Being an artistic director, too. I'd like that. For when... I can't do more of...this."

It's the big taboo. All "content creators" know that they probably won't do this for their whole lives, but no one dares to really talk about it.

To be honest, it scares me, too. I have no idea what I'm going to do "after." We'll see.

Our day's schedule is running like clockwork. I have to hand it to her. Mila is a production pro. Sam says I can learn a lot from her. He's right. He's always right. It annoys me.

"Can I ask you a weird question?" Mila says.

"Go ahead."

"What's Sam like, in real life?"

"..."

"I mean, before he met you he had a reputation for being quite the party guy, not super serious...

Now it looks like he's turned into the perfect man. Actually, you two are my couplegoals. I'm jealous."

She said couplegoals. Okay, I'm flattered. It makes me feel like I actually have my shit together all of a sudden. And it makes me want to be honest.

"It's nice of you to say that. It's true that he's changed quite a bit in a year. His friends often tell him that. But I only know the new Sam. He's a pretty intense guy. He thinks a lot about our careers...You know, it's funny, but I used to think that when I fell in love, it would mean I'd finally made it, I could settle in and start to enjoy life, but, um..."

Mila is looking at me funny. Why on earth did I just say that?

Bad move. I regroup.

"No, really, he's a great guy. He's so supportive of all my projects, it's really encouraging. I'm lucky. I hope you meet someone like that."

Mila's face looks normal again. Whew.

We film our four videos one after another, like a couple of machines.

It's a long workday, but I'm really happy with them. We have Mila's DIY fall decor, a very fun Q&A where we answer the most embarrassing questions from our fans, a recipe segment featuring pumpkin energy bars and to finish, I show Mila a few simple pre-bedtime stretches.

It's inspiring to make content as a team. And it's true that Mila has changed in the past eight years.

One more point for Sam.

As I gather up my makeup and four wardrobe changes, she says, "I'm going to an anti-bullying benefit concert on Friday. You could come. It's going to be amazing! They give out VIP passes in exchange for visibility. Just one post, nothing complicated. There'll be lots of YouTubers like us and a red carpet for photo ops."

"Uh, I don't think you want to do a red carpet with me. I'm pretty crappy at it."

"But it would be perfect for showing off our new collaboration and promoting our videos."

"I know . . . it's just that I get really stressed out and clumsy."

"There's nothing to it! I'll coach you a bit, and you'll get super good at it."

"Okay. That could be cool. Sam's going to be on tour, so, sure. I'm on board."

"Great! You won't regret it."

THROWBACK

The person who put the salad in front of my locker in senior year was Ariane Brunelle, Mila's best friend. She bragged about it in the locker room after a volleyball match where she had played particularly well. Maude Courteau's girlfriend heard her talking about it in front of the whole world. She passed the news on to An Nguyen, who told my friend Camille.

Camille decided to wait for the right time to tell me. She waited a very long time. I think she knew I would freak out.

She ended up spilling the beans after a fairly intense romantic-comedy movie marathon in my basement. She knew that I wouldn't be especially thrilled by the news.

I cried all night, curled up alone in a ball on the basement floor, listening to "Wonderwall" by Oasis. I ended up falling asleep from exhaustion around 4:00 a.m.

It sure didn't help knowing that during this whole time, Mila would chat away with me in art class like nothing had happened. As if her best friend wasn't in the middle of a bullying campaign against me.

When I found out, I stopped talking to her right away. She didn't even seem to notice. For days after I wondered what part she'd played in the whole salad business. Did she participate? Was it her idea? Was she going to tell Ariane everything we'd talked about in art class?

I went through all the scenarios in my head. Except I should have gone and asked her straight out instead of imagining a whole bunch of stuff.

Maybe that would have allowed us to avoid the "incident."

18

When he sees Sam and me arrive, Malik gets up. He opens his arms wide to welcome us.

I'm a bit taken aback, because it's unusual for him. I don't hate it.

"Mr. and Mrs. Quinoa Forever, the star couple! Make yourselves comfortable. Sparkling water? Coffee, tea? A grilled cheese?"

I say yes to sparkling water. Then we sit in the giant upholstered armchairs in front of his desk. We exchange a few pleasantries. We talk about the weather outside and Cath Bonenfant's last controversial video — a vlog where she admits that she has self-mutilated and received Botox injections.

Then there's silence. Malik takes his time, weighing each word before throwing it out.

"I'd like to represent both of you. Individually, of course, but also as a couple."

Sam instantly turns to me. I guess he wants to know what I think. But he doesn't look the least bit surprised.

Malik continues. "It's to our advantage to stop thinking of you as separate entities that evolve in parallel. We have to start thinking in terms of you as a couple and plan our strategy accordingly. The numbers clearly show that when you're together — wow — things explode. It's fireworks time."

I was expecting Malik to tell us that we'd received some big partnership offer as a couple, not suggesting that we develop a common strategy.

"Um, sure...it's an interesting idea. We can start to think about it, maybe talk about it some more."

The truth is, I'm semi tempted. Quinoa is the base of my business, but at the same time, I'm not going to be so boring that I stop my boyfriend from having a social-media career on top of his career as a musician. And it's true it will give me a leg up, too.

It's just...do we really have to merge? Is it really the thing to do?

In the space of one second, I imagine tossing my glass of sparkling water at the wall behind Malik.

I wonder how he'd react. How much noise it would make. The tiny bubbles of carbon dioxide exploding. The glass shattering and falling on the carpet. I think about how I would justify it. What I would say.

Malik's voice pulls me out of my thoughts.

"Excellent, excellent. Sam has put me in touch

with his management team. They're comfortable with our proposal. We manage Sam's influencer career but don't touch the music. That remains their department."

I have a funny feeling that I've missed some big clue.

"Oh, so you talked about this before? I would have —"

"We're talking to you now." This time it's Sam talking, speaking gently, with a big smile. "I wanted to make sure that it was possible before telling you. So you wouldn't be disappointed if it didn't work out. It's super good news, eh?"

I tell myself yes. That if Sam and Malik think that it's a good idea, it must be a good idea...

Except I have a hard time believing that 100 percent.

"I feel like we're going to go far together," Malik says. "Your last video was already right on the mark. A perfect combination of romance, humor and intimacy with the added bonus of a recipe and a touch of soft porn. Honestly, I rarely say this, but I was very impressed. And the reaction — wow! They want more. Especially girls between 25 and 34. It's absolutely essential that we stay on this trajectory."

Sam takes my hand and squeezes it super tight. I can tell he's really enthusiastic. So much so that I feel bad for having doubts.

"Congratulations, Ellie," Malik continues. "With all the hype around you two over the past seventy-two hours, you've officially crossed the 500,000 subscriber mark. Your publisher already wants to do a follow-up to your book. Welcome to the top. You've made it!"

You've made it.

I smile. This is bigger than me. I have 500,000 subscribers. Five hundred thousand. Five times a hundred thousand. Half a million. Finished sixth in the rankings. Finito. And that — I have to admit it — is in large part thanks to Sam.

"Do you know why your relationship comes across so well on the web?" Malik asks, smiling.

Sam opens his mouth to answer, but Malik jumps in. "Because people love to believe that their life could be just like one of those ridiculous bedtime stories they tell children to get them to sleep. You, Ellie, you're like the ugly duckling turned into a swan, and you, Sam, the big beast transformed into

Prince Charming. You two are like a fairy tale on steroids. A magic wand slash snake oil for social media. The proof is that since Tuesday, I've been receiving new advertising partnership proposals for you every hour. We're already talking six figures."

Our eyes are as round as marbles. It's my turn to squeeze Sam's hand super tight.

Malik rests his elbows on the table before continuing.

"I have something a little radical to propose..."

"Okay. What?"

"We refuse the offers. All of them."

I gasp. It's unthinkable to turn down that much money. Especially when I have no small amount to pay off on my credit card before the end of the month because of the move and new furniture we ordered.

Meanwhile, Sam is trying to formulate a coherent sentence.

"Um well, I...don't think —"

Malik interrupts. "We'll let the bidding go up. We make it clear to advertisers that you are luxury goods. And we wait. To begin with, we want at least one big, juicy partnership. No more small contracts with two or three posts here and there. We want something substantial, a main sponsor. I think you're ready for the next stage, and we need to plan accordingly. And if we play our cards right, you, Ellie, could be much more than just an influencer."

"More...?"

"Much more. Quinoa Forever could become a brand."

A *brand*.

With a sweep of his hand, Malik says the word "brand" like he's talking about a shooting star. His eyes gleam as he continues.

"Instead of being good little lapdogs who sell other people's products, we sell your own stuff! We position you two as the perfect model of great romantic love and, poof! In a few months, adolescent girls and their mothers will want to buy anything from you!"

"What exactly would that mean?"

"Just use a little imagination! A collection of clothing, a magazine, ready-to-eat meals, emojis, kitchenware, lingerie, diet pills, makeup, playlists, athletic footwear, a web series, yoga studios, workout machines, herbal teas — anything you want. Quinoa

Forever, a veritable empire of romance and well-being. With you, Ellie, a triumphant idol on the arm of the man of your dreams, Samuel Vanasse, accomplished musician and lover."

Sam's eyes sparkle. He finally manages to get a word in edgewise.

"Yes! We're on the same wavelength. By combining our strengths, anything is possible. To the top, baby!"

"Well said, Samuel! Good. So, creating a successful brand from a social-media phenomenon is extremely difficult from a business point of view. Like doing a back flip from influencer marketing. But I'm here to help you. First of all, Sam, you sign here, here and here."

Malik hands contracts to Sam, who grabs a pen.

"Okay, here's the plan, my chicks. Listen up."

**Top 10 YouTubers
CAN/FR**

1. Jordanne Jacques – 803,400 followers
2. Tellement Cloé – 761,100 followers
3. Emma & Juju – 504,070 followers
4. Cath Bonenfant – 502,800 followers
5. **Ellie - Quinoa Forever – 500,800 followers**
6. Mila Mongeau – 499,250 followers
7. Approved by Gwen – 426,600 followers
8. Sophie Chen – 341,500 followers
9. Maëla Djeb – 160,500 followers
10. Zoé around the World – 143,500 followers

David Lanctôt has sent you a Facebook message

D: Sorry to bother you with this, Quinoa, but it's a bit of an emergency. I made your kale detox smoothie recipe with avocado and ginger. But am I supposed to drink it or put it in my bath? The bath, right?

E: Yes, that's it. Very important to rub it in well behind the ears.

D: OK, thanks.

D: So I guess the guy with you in your morning routine video, he's your boyfriend, right?

E: Yes. Right.

D: Cool.

E: Yup.

D: Great.

E: And you, David Lanctôt, how are you?

D: Perfecto.

E: No, but for real?

19

This morning Sam and I are shooting a video that my fans have been waiting for for a long time: the *boyfriend tag*. I get asked for it at least once a day since I started going out with him, but I wanted to wait until we were living together. I've seen so many You-Tubers change the title of their videos to *EX-boyfriend tag* not long after putting theirs online. It's so sad.

But now the timing is perfect.

We settle into the living room. I've prepared a list of surprise questions. Sam has no idea what's in store for him. It's funny already.

I turn on my camera, my lighting, make some adjustments and sit down next to him on our beautiful new green velvet sofa.

"Hi, everyone! I hope you're doing well! Today Sam and I are making a video that a lot of you have asked me for: the *boyfriend tag*. Okay, here we go. I'm pumped. Are you ready, Sam?"

"Bring it on."

"This doesn't stress you out at all?"

"Not at all."

"Not even a teensy bit?"

"No, my cupcake."

My cupcake. He's never called me that before. It's cute. He kisses me. I read the first question off my phone.

"Which of us made the first move?"

"That would be me."

"Well, I'm the one who ran into you."

"Did you do it on purpose?"

"No, but —"

"Good. It was me. I invited you to dinner!"

"I admit it. It was you." I give Sam a little peck on the cheek, then scroll down to choose the next question.

"Ah, this one. I can't wait to find out. What was your first impression of me?"

"The truth is, Ellie, I got a hard-on."

"EXCUSE ME?!"

"What's the matter?"

"Are you kidding me? A hard-on? I can't record that."

"Why not?"

"Come on. It's...vulgar!"

"It's not vulgar, it's true." Sam raises a finger in the air and adds, "Malik would say I'm being *authentic.*"

"Yeah, but my sponsor is bound to find it inappropriate, smartass." I sigh a thousand times before going on. "So your first impression of me was that I was…"

"That you were really beautiful."

"That's it?"

"Well, that's good, isn't it?"

"Hmmm…My first impression of *you* was that you were charismatic, not shy, brilliant and also really charming. Even more so in real life than on screen."

Sam looks surprised but flattered.

I feel weird knowing that all he thought the first time we saw each other was that I was beautiful. It makes me happy, too, but, it's like…too simple.

"Which of the new flavors of Kombudream could I drink every day?"

"Um. Turmeric chai?"

"Totally! And I like lemon mint a lot. Argh, it's so hard to just choose one. Write in the comments which is your favorite. I really want to know."

We go through the other questions. I've written out so many that we can just keep the best ones. After about ten or so, I decide on one last question.

"What do you think my dream wedding would

look like? Simple or extravagant?"

"You want to get married?"

"Well, maybe. Yes."

Sam says nothing.

I burst out laughing.

"Oops. Awkward."

"No, no. It's just that I don't know! I would say simple, but in a very Pinterest kind of way, with lots of ferns, gold accents and garlands of lights everywhere."

"Ferns!"

"You know what I mean. It's your style. Admit it."

"I admit it. I'm in love with you, my love."

"You are my beautiful girlfriend."

We kiss for a really long time for the camera.

I think it makes a nice ending.

AD

People often ask how much I get paid for a post. The answer is that it depends.

I would say that there are two kinds of partnerships. Those with brands that I give credibility to, like Glow Cosmetics or Bubble drinks. That's more expensive.

And there are partnerships with brands that give me credibility, like Summit Athletica or Joie Paris — prestige brands that I'm happy to be associated with. That make me look good. That costs a little less.

The price also depends on the kind of content they're asking for. A story is cheaper than a post, which is cheaper than a video. Other elements to take into consideration are how the brand wants me to present its product. If I have to show it in its packaging, it's more expensive. If I'm not allowed to integrate other brands in my publication, it's more expensive. If they want an exclusivity clause, it's more expensive. And then the price also varies depending on the number of subscribers to my pages. I don't charge the same price now that I have 250,000 followers on Instagram as I did when I had 40,000.

I'm sure I'm forgetting things, but I have an agent who takes care of that now. It's way easier than when I was working out of my living room.

One thing that I find a bit weird is that the line between reality and fiction becomes more and more blurry. Take the partnerships, for instance. Before, back when people watched TV, all publicity was done by the big agencies. You paid the writers, directors, artistic directors, actors — a whole ream of people — to advertise. Then everyone understood that it was staged. That these were not real people. I mean, everyone knew that the people doing ads on television weren't real.

But today when I say that PURE After-Sun Beauty Balm is the best thing that ever happened to my skin this summer, or when I'm shown loving life while eating a Yaourti peach yogurt before dawn, I'm not sure it's clear that this isn't real-real. It's also not false! I mean, I would never say I like something when I don't. But, for $25,000, I think anyone would fall in love with their espresso machine. Probably even to the point of talking about it in five stories, three posts and two videos.

It's funny, there are cases when I no longer know

whether I do things because I feel like it, or whether they help me showcase products. That's the biz, when I think about it.

Hey, but that's okay, right? Anyway, this is how things work now, and if I don't do them, someone else will.

20

We're having dinner with my father tonight. I'm looking for something to wear. I've tried on ten thousand things and can't find anything I like. Except maybe a black wraparound V-neck dress, but I'm not sure. I call Sam for backup.

When he comes into the bedroom, I casually try to suck in my stomach, and I place my foot at an angle. God knows why, but I've always thought this pose worked for me.

"What do you think of the dress?"

Sam examines me carefully. He takes his role very seriously. It's cute.

"Honestly, Ellie, you look extremely yummy in that dress."

He grabs me by the waist and nibbles my earlobe, making munching sounds. I laugh. But I'm not convinced. I want to look flawless in front of my father.

We haven't seen each other for a long time and I want to make an impression. So he sees that I'm doing well. That I'm successful, and don't need his help.

"Are you telling the truth? It's not a bit too ordinary?"

Sam presses his erection against my butt.

"Feel how sincere I am."

"Hmm. Wow, I like that, it's so...authentic."

Sam doesn't seem to get the joke. Never mind. I can't resist him any longer, and I melt into his arms. He gives me a deep kiss. I'm excited. He slips his hands over my breasts and down over my hips.

When he gets to my stomach, he stops.

"Oh, look out, I think I found where you hid my peanut butter cookies."

It takes me a good three seconds to understand, and I push him away.

"What did you just say?"

"Hey, I'm kidding..."

"Okay, so you seriously think I stuffed my face with your cookies and didn't tell you?"

"Come on, Ellie, it was a joke. Forget it."

Sam tries to take me in his arms again, but I stop him.

"Forget what? I told you I never saw those cookies. Plus they're packed with refined sugar. Like I would have eaten them."

"Please, can you just let it go..."

He wants to pick up where we left off, but I'm not

in the mood anymore. I want to ask him if he still thinks I'm beautiful, if he thinks I've put on weight.

But what comes out of my mouth is, "Just say it, you think I look like a fat cow who stuffs her face with junk food all day long! Don't be shy, go on!"

"Ellie, you're freaking out, okay? It was a JOKE."

Sam takes his head in his hands. He looks upset. After a long sigh, he lies down on the bed and puts a pillow over his head.

I don't understand how this happened. I sit on the bed, disheartened. I stare at my feet and wait for him to say something. But he doesn't.

I feel really guilty. It was just a joke, right? We could have discussed it calmly. I hate it when my emotions take over like that. It's like I turn into another person. It's not nice.

"I'm sorry, Sam. I've had a big week. I shouldn't have reacted like that."

"'Kay."

"We can go out for a drink after dinner. It would be good to spend some time together, just the two of us."

Sam takes the pillow off his head.

"Yeah...well, not sure I really want to go to dinner after...that."

"But…it's been organized so I can introduce you to my father. You can't not be there."

"Don't take this the wrong way, Ellie, but I really am tired. I've been sleeping really badly for two nights, and this…thing has taken everything out of me. I think it would be better if I pass."

I can feel my heart beating in my temples. Sam talks without looking at me.

"We'll do it another time. Anyway, this dinner is for your sister. You don't really want to introduce me to your father, admit it."

"Okay, I admit it, but…"

"It's okay. We'll do it again soon, I promise."

"Geez. I can't believe you're doing this to me! I know my father. He'll think you don't really love me and that I just can't see it!"

Sam takes two whole seconds to take this in before saying, "Why don't you show him the articles in *Celebrity World*?"

I made a big effort not to cry my eyes out in the taxi between the apartment and the restaurant. Failed. My face is one big smear of tears. Even after spending at least forty minutes getting ready. I have to make a detour through the pharmacy to save my face. Refresh my makeup with the samples on the counter.

An old trick. As long as the cosmetician doesn't catch on.

I walk past the shampoos and medications to the cosmetics at the back. It gives me a little head start. I take a tester of fairly pale foundation, pretend to look at what's written on the label. I spot a mirror not too close to the counter. I dip my finger in the bottle and dab a little under my eyes to cover up traces of mascara. It doesn't camouflage much. I take a subtle glance at the cosmetician.

She's busy with a client. Good. I try to look like I'm just casually shopping, but I'm desperately looking for a matte powder tester.

I find one. With my fingers I put it on my nose and under my eyes. I'm discreetly replacing the compact when the cosmetician, a very petite lady of about sixty-five, comes to ask if I need any help.

"Thanks," I say, forcing a smile. "But I'm just looking."

"No problem. Poor pumpkin, your mascara is running. Come on, I'll fix it for you."

Denise, her nametag tells me, sits me down in an overstuffed chair ramped up way too high. With her little foot, she pumps the lever several times to bring me down to her height. She takes some large cotton balls and makeup remover to clean up the disaster under my eyes.

After a few minutes, she says, very seriously, "I'll tell you something that just old broads like me know. When you're young, you spend your time convincing yourself that everything is okay. You'll do everything in your power not to hear the little voice that tells you what you don't want to hear. Right? You know what I'm talking about! But that little voice, my girl, is your best friend. You should listen to it more often!"

I smile. She's cute, Denise, with her big truths about life. I imagine her giving out advice on You-Tube. She'd be good at it. I'd subscribe to her channel, that's for sure.

Then I think back to Sam. His annoyed look. My

eyes fill up again, but this time, luckily, I stop them from brimming over.

Denise pretends not to notice. It's nice of her. She applies a bit of concealer, powder, mascara.

Then, with a sly look, she says, "A little lipstick?"

"Okay."

Denise carefully opens one of the large drawers of the PURE display, like it's her personal treasure chest. She fingers through a row of small gold tubes before landing on the right one. Satisfied, she uses a small brush to apply cherry red color to my lips.

"Gorgeous! Make the most of it. Being sensible is for old hags like me."

Denise winks at me. Sensible? Denise? I don't believe it for two seconds.

After thanking her profusely and buying the lipstick, I go back down the shampoo aisle and look at myself in the mirrors that are for sale.

Ooh la la! Denise went all out with cherry. It's cute. I blot my lips with my coat sleeve. My eyes are green from crying too much. They change color when I'm sad. I think it's beautiful.

I take a selfie. Then two, then three. The eleventh one isn't bad.

I quickly retouch the photo with Facetune. I open my Notes app. I copy and paste a small text that I composed last week. I fix it so it fits a little with the photo.

Then I post my selfie on Instagram before hurrying past the cash to leave the pharmacy.

♡ ◯ ↑

12 043 Likes

ellie_quinoa_forever Just a little basic selfie I took at the pharmacy to remind myself that we all need positive energy. Because energy is contagious. BIG TIME. We have to know how to surround ourselves with people who help us to be the best version of ourselves. Who have a positive influence. This is the best medicine. ❤ **#selfcare #goodvibes #TeamEllie**

See all 98 comments

nathan_b No matter what, you influence me positively with your beauty.

loulou_mo Ellie, tonight, YOU touch me . . . What beautiful words, which I take seriously, to change myself and my surroundings . . . YOU are a magnificent inspiration. Thank you!

maelle_siou Is it me or has she gained weight **@jezabelbernier** ??

Ari_2001 Ellie!! I can't believe how beautiful you are!!! I love it! You've motivated me to start training again. This time it feels right. GO GO GO! ❤

essbad22 Hahahah @ antoinelambert4 you like it????

fabiola42 You are magnificent, your beauty is resplendent even apart from your looks!

rosevigneault Omg you're sooooo beautiful!!!!!! I ❤ you so much. I've been following your program of healthy recipes to the letter for two weeks with great results ❤ ❤ ❤ ❤ #proud #TeamEllie

fleurfleurfleur Inspiring!!! I would so love to have your body!

marie_joelle You are such a good influence damn I love you #TeamEllie

clara_lacroix_ We want photos of Sam!

alexe1808 A winner.

mathildenpp WOW what you write is truly beautiful and so true you are so beautiful

claudellemicho Wow where did you find your toque?

julieanne STUNNING #TeamEllie

vis_ta_vie_12 Well said! I was wondering, what do you think I should eat for lunch? I don't like eggs. Thank you!

sylvainflamand2016 Mmmm YOU are sublime xxxx

claudepel As for me, I'd really like to be a positive influence on you ;-) **@ellie_quinoa_forever**

eric_limoges_actor Wow what an amazing pic! You're an angel.

jessica_aube_00 You are a real fighter. So inspiring. So motivating! Love ya!!!

elody.cloudier @ellie_quinoa_forever When is your book coming out??? I'm dying for one. I really have to get my hands on one LOL.

22

When I get to the restaurant I'm struck by the fact that Alice is wearing real clothes. Not her usual shapeless and ironic laundry-day style but a navy pleated skirt and a shirt.

I should take it as a warning. Make a run for it. Flee. Because Alice's seemingly innocuous decision to renounce her usual wardrobe style is a sign of all the betrayal to come.

But, innocent as I am, I pull out the chair next to my sister while nicely saying hello to Jacques, my father.

We haven't seen each other in a year.

He's aged. His face is full of wrinkles. His shoulders are hunched. His eyelids droop. Gray tufts sprout from his nostrils and ears.

The only discordant element is his hair, black as ebony.

I suppress a smile. He's dyeing his hair. My mother would laugh. She's always thought that men coloring their hair is grotesque.

Alice interrupts her conversation with my father to welcome me.

"Ellie, hi! Sam's not with you?"

I've practiced my answer two thousand times in my head. It comes out super natural.

"No, something came up. An emergency. A song he has to rearrange before the tour. He was so disappointed not to be able to come."

"Oh, that really sucks," Alice says quickly. "We never get to see him, this handsome Samuel Vanasse. Papa, Sam's a singer. He was on *The Voice*. It's a *reality show* on TV." She insists on making finger quotes around the words "reality show."

While my father gets up to give me a kiss, Alice makes big eyes at me behind his back. As if Sam's absence is going to ruin her plan. I feel like telling her to just calm down but I smile so my father doesn't notice anything.

"Wow, Élisabeth, you're melting away like snow on a sunny day! We're finally seeing the beautiful young woman that was hiding inside you!"

The intended positive comments about my weight loss really make me uncomfortable. Is it just me, or does it sound more like an insult than a compliment?

My father carries on. "Your mother must be happy. I hardly recognized you."

He's laughing. His laugh makes me want to scratch the table with my fingernails. Not that I'd forgotten how much I hate spending time with my father, but I didn't realize the reminder would be so brutal.

"Thanks, Papa."

With a bit too much enthusiasm, Alice starts to tell my father all about my accomplishments over the past year.

"Did you know that Ellie has become an internet star? It's wild. She earns a living with YouTube videos! She doesn't even need a real job, can you imagine? Because she has thousands of followers, companies pay her to promote their products like shampoo or energy bars. Maman and I are really proud of her. It's so hot!"

I stare at Alice, aghast. What is she doing? First, I know she doesn't mean a single word of what she's just said. And second, she knows that I avoid talking about my career with my father at all costs. It's no secret that having a daughter who earns a livelihood from YouTube is nothing short of a parental tragedy.

You need to know that the eminent Jacques Marois, my dear papa, is a professor of literature, specializing in the work of Dostoevsky. When I was nine he forced me to read authors like Jules Verne and Marcel Pagnol. At the age of eleven, I had to take extra summer courses in French to "improve my spelling and enrich my vocabulary." At twelve, it was Saturday lessons in Latin.

After that, he just gave up. Despite all his efforts, I remained a fairly average student. Even ordinary, unlike Alice.

I have never lived up to the intellectual aspirations that he had for me.

My father scrunches his eyebrows and says something like, "Well, that sounds..."

"I'm having a book published, too," I add, faced with his lack of enthusiasm.

A glimmer of hope, but Alice is quick to clarify. "A cookbook! Her protein smoothies are awesome."

My father stares at the restaurant floor.

"That's the way it works with technology today," Alice continues. "Everything is possible. You don't have to spend a long time studying. Look at me, for example, I could do a TikTok about something to do with selfcare and get super rich. Okay, for starters, maybe it would help to find a famous boyfriend like Samuel Vanasse and for me to stop eating carbs."

I glare at my sister. The last thing Alice wants is to

have a TikTok account and follow a diet. That would be her idea of hell.

While my father starts to look more depressed than ever, Alice goes in for the kill.

"You can't be an influencer after you get to be thirty or thirty-five, max, but anyway, given the way of the world, we have to take life one day at a time. That's what Maman always tells us."

Wow. Alice has scored big time. My father is practically at the boiling point. I feel like he's getting ready to dish out another sermon on the intellectual vacuousness of our time.

I don't have the stomach to listen to it, so I quickly slip away to the bathroom. I take deep breaths in front of the sink to calm down.

I don't know what stops me from defending my life choices. I always fall apart in front of my father.

I feel like such a failure.

I come back to the table just in time to see him hand my sister a big check. Given Alice's determination, I knew it was a possibility, but I never thought it would happen before the main course.

I can see fireworks exploding in her eyes. She is ecstatic.

I listen to my father and Alice talk for more than an hour. It looks like they're making a point of choosing impossible topics for discussion. But I'm not a fool. I could talk about lots of things...if they gave me the chance.

I wonder what it would have been like if Sam had come. I tell myself they would have made an effort to include *him* in the conversation.

After the main course, my father takes on a look that's half solemn, half relaxed.

"I don't want to worry you girls," he says. "But I've been having some...abdominal discomfort lately. Probably benign tumors in the intestine. Nothing serious. I'm having surgery in two weeks. Routine procedure. No need to talk about it to your mother."

I try to look concerned and compassionate. I hope it works, because I'm not really feeling it. Alice is quick to ask if she can go with him to the hospital. The opportunity is too good to pass up. If it weren't for her urgent need for financial support over the next three years, I don't know if she would have volunteered.

I try to make an effort, but all this hypocrisy is starting to weigh heavy on my heart. I spend the rest of the dinner with my nose in my plate and wait for it to end. I check about fifteen times to see if Sam has texted. Alice takes care of the conversation.

Seeing that I'm sulking in my corner, my father tries to cheer me up.

"Have a little crème brûlée, Élisabeth. It will do you good to eat. We wouldn't want you to disappear altogether!"

I say nothing. I take a spoonful of crème brûlée to keep the peace. Wonder how many calories there are in it. My father winks at me. He asks for the bill. Calls a cab. I give him a peck on each cheek. My sister gives him a big tender hug before he gets into his taxi.

23

Alice falls to her knees on the sidewalk.

"YES! YESSS! YESSSS!" she shouts, her arms to the sky. She's on cloud nine.

I want to strangle her.

"The fact is, right from the start, your plan was to use me to convince Papa to pay your tuition, right?"

Alice pulls a flask out of her coat. She takes a big swallow of alcohol.

"Hey, it's nothing against you. I exploited his weak spot. It was brilliant, admit it."

She offers me a sip of gin, which I refuse.

"So I'm his weak point? The failure daughter?"

"Ellie! Relax, you know that's not it. It's his problem, not yours."

My sister speaks to me in her usual voice of a girl who is used to getting whatever she wants from everyone. It bugs me.

"Seriously, Alice, I know that you're completely self-centered, and that it's hard for you to put yourself in the place of others, but that was really going too far."

"Come on. I didn't realize it would be such a hardship —"

"Oh, forget it, Alice. Save your bullshit for someone else."

I start to walk. Alice follows me.

"So now you're going to sulk, Ellie? We have something to celebrate!"

I turn around to face her.

"Did you honestly not think for a single second how it would make me feel to know once again that I mean less than nothing to Papa? Huh? For a single second?"

"No…"

"Well, there you have it. There's only one person who counts for anything in the life of Alice Bourdon-Marois, and that's Alice Bourdon-Marois. Goodnight."

Stung, Alice follows me down the sidewalk.

"Hey! Excuse me, Ellie," she says, super loud and waving her arms. "But I don't think it's a crime to point out that posting selfies and videos of your morning routine on social media is not EXACTLY a life vocation!"

I whip back around to face her.

"And to sign up for a sociology degree because you've got a thing for your prof — is that a life project? Like, have you thought about how many students like you he screws in a year, your handsome Jeff? Starting with your roommates. So don't come and lecture me about my life choices."

I had no idea I thought that. But I clearly do.

I pick up my pace, and Alice stops following me.

I may have gone a bit far, but I've never felt better.

OBSESSED

I've started to do this thing...it's funny to admit, but sometimes to fall asleep at night, I think about Dave. I replay our conversations over and over in my head. I think back to everything we've ever said to each other. About his eyes when he looks at me. His voice. His shoulders. And I make up lots of stories for us, about whatever. I imagine he's here, and I fall asleep.

Other times during the day I wonder what it would be like if he was here. What he would say. What we would do. What he would think about the way I wash the dishes or brush my teeth.

I think of Dave and it feels good. I love the person I am when he's around. Even if it's just in my head.

Then when that's not enough, I find an excuse to go on Facebook. I've become an expert in the art of pretending that I'm not trying to see if he's sent me a message. That I am not typing his name in the Search bar. I go to his profile. I sneak peeks at his picture. Like I'm afraid he'll see me doing it.

Then I quit the page.

Or sometimes I'm more reckless. I dig into his profile looking for clues about his life. I spy on people who like his posts. I wonder if he's dating. Which girls he finds beautiful. Who he's thinking about before he falls asleep.

But I don't tell anyone about this.

It's ridiculous. It'll pass.

Email from Malik to Ellie and Samuel

Subject: Karma - Main Sponsor

The wolf has entered the fold, my friends. Everything is going as planned. First step: check. We have our big, juicy partnership. Jean-Félix will send you two copies of the contract for signatures. Get them back to us quickly.

Talk soon!

Samuel Vanasse sent you a Facebook message

S: I found your recipe for maca energy balls on Pinterest and I made two dozen. I hope you aren't too mad at me about dinner. I love you. See you next week.

Miss U already.

24

Mother-daughter yoga. Virabhadrasana III. I hold the pose, but my mind is elsewhere. In fact, my head is completely in the clouds.

Malik was right. His plan is working beautifully. We've reached a partnership agreement with Karma. They specialize in organic, vegan and gluten-free products.

It's so hot. I am officially the new face of the brand. Which is PERFECT, because I adore their products.

We start in full force with a Christmas campaign. There's going to be a microsite entirely devoted to "Ellie and Sam's Vegan Christmas," with recipe videos, a full-page photo spread in *Femme* magazine, a pre-roll ad on YouTube and even a TV commercial.

I'm ecstatic. So much so that I forget that I'm still balancing on one leg. I wobble, fall on my hands and roll like a ball onto my neighbor's mat, which makes her fall, too.

Oops. She looks a bit angry.

Alexandra, my mother's new "favorite" yoga teacher, rushes over to help me get up.

"Breathe. Calm your mind. Ooooommmm."

"I'm really sorry..."

"Uttanasana, Forward Fold."

Good. First step: plan a vegan Christmas menu using as many Karma products as possible. Second step: film the recipe videos. Last step: host the whole family for a Christmas photo shoot.

Karma will take care of decorating our DIY-style apartment. Firs, garlands, candles, wreaths, centerpieces...I saw them on their Pinterest board. It's going to be unbelievably beautiful.

I have two weeks to wrap this up. Which is funny, because it's still October. The first person I have to convince to help me, and quick, is my mother. She's bound to have some ideas. I wanted to talk to her about it this morning, but she didn't come to class. I thought I saw her arrive late, and I was looking forward to giving her the death stare for once. I even had a comment prepared to tease her.

Except she never showed up...

She must have a good reason.

I spend all of the final relaxation trying to come up with a festive starter made with walnuts and flax.

If Alexandra only knew how much is spinning in my head right now, she would rush over to sprinkle a few essential oils on me.

Oops, I just laughed out loud. Hope no one heard.

I pretend to cough to cover my tracks.

∞

When I come out of the yoga studio, my mother's car is parked in front of the door.

Okay, this is too weird. It's hers. I recognize the pineapple-shaped air freshener hanging from the rearview mirror.

I call her on her cell but get her voicemail.

Should I be worried? Did we maybe cross paths without seeing each other? Could I have come too early?

Impossible, Nico's class is the one that starts now, and my mother categorically refuses to attend those. She prefers the "soothing feminine energy of Alexandra." No comment.

I go to the café next door. Empty. I go back to the studio. No trace of my mother. Not in the locker room, either. At the reception, I ask Alexandra if Estelle Bourdon signed up for a class today, saying she's my mother and that her car is out front.

She looks at her iPad very, very slowly.

"She was enrolled in the 8:15, just like you."

I try to stay rational, but I start to seriously consider the possibility of a kidnapping.

In an extraordinarily calm voice, Alexandra says, "You can always check out the small studio upstairs, next to the men's locker room. There are private classes there from time to time."

A private lesson is highly unlikely, but I still climb the stairs in turbo mode, my cell in my hands. I tell myself that the next step is to make an emergency call to Alice.

The door is closed and the lights are out. It's obvious there's no one here.

Still, I open the door just to check.

Mistake. Big mistake.

In the light filtering from the corridor, I see something that will remain stamped on my retinas forever. My mother and Nico, feverishly embracing, half naked, making out like there's no tomorrow.

I can't take my eyes off the scene. I stand there like a fool long enough for them to see me. It is awkward on an intergalactic scale.

"Excuse me, I'm looking for … the car … I was in the …"

My mother laughs like a kid. I know her well enough to know that she's glad I'm here to witness her little romp in the hay, her rediscovered youth, her improbable conquest.

Nico quickly puts his sweater back on. Says he's late for his class. Gives my mother a last kiss on the mouth before walking past me and down to the ground floor.

My mother pulls on her tights.

"And you're the one who always told me to knock before coming in," she says proudly.

"Oh, Maman!"

How many years of therapy will it take for me to recover from this?

Many. Thousands, at least.

David Lanctôt has sent you a Facebook message

E: No, but for real?

D: For real? Big question ;)

E: Nothing to lose. We'll probably never see each other
again . . .

D: Ha ha. Good one. Better than last time. I have more help
at the café, gives me time to breathe. Go see my nephew.
Maybe even do some small renovations!

E: Ah, cool! Happy for you.

D: But that would be boring.

E: What?

D: To never see each other again.

25

Tonight's the anti-bullying benefit concert. Mila offered to come to my house so we could get ready together. I'm so afraid of being too much or not quite enough, tripping over my shoes or looking like a deer caught in the headlights in the photos...

So much so that I haven't slept in two days. That, and the fact that Sam went on tour with his band for a week the day before yesterday. He gives a concert tonight in Toronto, then after that it's Chicago, Minneapolis and Ottawa. They play small rooms for now, but his career is really taking off.

I'm super happy for him. It's just...

I have a funny feeling. He left before we really had a chance to talk about our fight. And now he's super far away, surrounded by lots of groupies...

I trust him, it's not that. He's told me a thousand times how much he's so over one-night stands with fans. And I really want to let him have his moment. Let him be in his "tour bubble."

But at the same time, I'd like to talk to each other and feel that everything is okay with us. Because there's like a cloud that weighs heavy on my heart whenever I think of him.

I am spreading out possible outfits on my bed when Mila rings the bell. I look at myself quickly in the mirror before going to let her in. I try to look relaxed while I walk down the hall. I know she can see me through the leaf design etched in the glass.

I open the door. Mila is pulling a big wheelie suitcase, wearing round smoky glasses and holding a giant coffee in her right hand.

It's funny to see her in my doorway. If someone had told me at the end of high school that one day Mila Mongeau and I would be getting ready together to fight against bullying, I'd probably have had a heart attack.

Mila throws me a knowing look over her glasses.

"Stressed?" she asks.

"Mmmmhmmm."

"Oh my God."

"What?"

"It's a good thing I came."

She rolls her suitcase to my room and opens it on my bed. It's so full that as soon as it's unzipped, the contents balloon out and fall over the sides.

She lays a pile of clothes on my pillow, throws three pairs of sneakers on the floor, then starts tossing out big Ziploc bags full of small bottles of hairspray, baby powder, wipes, cotton swabs, sticky tape, false eyelashes, and a ton of makeup tubes and cases.

Looking inside them, she asks, "Sleep well?"

"Not really."

She grabs a bundle of anti-wrinkle patches and sticks them under my eyes.

"Me neither."

Then, pointing at my clothes on the bed, "Is that what you're going to wear?"

"Uh... those were possibilities."

"They're cute, but I don't think it's that kind of formal event. Maybe a shirtdress, but I'd even avoid that."

"Oh. Okay."

Mila pulls out a pink miniskirt and a loose washed-out crop top from her pile of clothes.

"More like this kind of vibe. This is what I'm going to wear. Do you want me to go through your things?"

Mila dives into my closet. Eyebrows furrowed, she flips through the hangers one by one like she's on some grand scientific mission to save humanity. She stops in front of a white jersey jumpsuit.

"This one!"

"Okay."

"It's very beautiful."

"Meh…"

I actually love this outfit. The thing is that I weighed myself this morning. I'm pretty much above my "ideal weight." It's not really a great situation for a red carpet.

Damn it. What's happening to me? One thing is certain, I'm going to look like a potato in this outfit.

"It's gotten too small for me."

"Oh, right. Damn washing machine, eh?"

"No, it's not that…"

There's a long, uneasy silence. I should have gone with the washing-machine explanation.

Clearly, the suggestion about my weight is not doing the trick. So instead I try being totally honest.

"I've gained weight. I guess it shows. Anyway, a few of my fans have noticed." I make a big disappointed face to show that I can laugh about it. So Mila thinks I'm okay with it.

Except instead she seems to feel bad for me. Shit.

"God, no! It doesn't show at all. They made comments, is that it? It makes me so mad, that kind of thing. You have the right to have whatever body you choose. Right?" She's speaking just a bit too loud. She's trying to be reassuring, but it feels forced.

"Yes, but it's clear I don't have 'the body I would choose' right now," I say, a bit annoyed.

"Sure, sure. I understand."

"I stick to my diet, eat healthy, work out, all that… but I gain weight anyway."

"Don't worry about it, Ellie, it's not important."

I know she's trying to be nice, but this bothers me even more.

"But you clearly pay a lot of attention to your weight, too, don't you?" I continue.

"Of course! Dear God. If you only knew."

"So…"

"What?"

"So, it *is* important. You wouldn't make so many sacrifices if you didn't think it was important to have a 'perfect' body, I mean."

"Ah, but it's a personal choice. I feel better like this, but I don't judge others. I'm in favor of body diversity. Aren't you?"

I'm uncomfortable with this double standard on body diversity. I know I'm on a slippery slope here, but I can't resist. I want to back her into a corner.

"Explain it to me, okay? I really want to understand. You say it's okay to have any kind of body, but *you* still want your own body to conform to a certain image of an ideal body type. To the point that you work really hard to achieve it. Right? And you talk a lot in your videos about your breast implants. I mean...when we see photos of you in a bikini or where you're wearing mini shorts that show off your butt, it's super beautiful but...admit that you're reinforcing the stereotype of the ideal body."

"..."

"Like, I'm not sure the girls who follow you feel like they can have just any body type. You know what I mean?"

"Yeah, maybe..."

It makes me feel good to throw it back in her face. Like taking a bit of revenge on behalf of the girls who have suffered for such a long time comparing themselves to the Milas of the world.

She shrugs. "But when I publish those photos, it's a kind of celebration of myself. An act of self-love. I don't do it for others, but just for myself. Do you understand? It shouldn't make people feel insecure. A girl has the right to feel good about herself and show it, I think..."

"…"

I don't know what to say. I disagree. I think if she was really doing this just for herself, she wouldn't need to put her photos on social media. And I don't think it has anything to do with self-confidence, either. I think those are two different things.

But I don't say anything. It's safer that way.

"You, too, Ellie, by the way," Mila adds, putting on her sneakers.

"Me, too, what?"

"You reinforce the stereotype, too. I know you feel bad because you've gained weight right now, and it's a delicate subject, but, like, I'm not the one selling detox recipes and exercise routines. You've become popular by losing weight. And you have the right to do so! I'm just saying that if I'm part of the problem, then so are you."

I take this like a slap in the face. I'm part of the problem? No! I want to tell her that it's really not the same thing. That I'm helping girls feel good, except…

Suddenly I'm not sure. The photos of Mila in a bikini and my sugar-free cookie recipes — are they really the same thing?

No, absolutely not. It's different with me. Completely different.

"No hard feelings," Mila says.

"Of course, no hard feelings!"

I tell myself that she can't understand... She's always been beautiful. Anyway, I need her help too much right now. I don't know what came over me.

Mila puts on her skirt and top.

"You should put this on," she says, looking at me in the mirror. She grabs a pair of faded jeans and throws them to me. "With Sam's band's T-shirt tied in front and your platform shoes."

"Great."

While I pull them on, Mila lies on the bed and leans on her elbows.

"The plan is to have our photo taken together on the red carpet. With luck it'll create some big buzz for the release of our videos."

"Good idea. And how do we do that?"

"Remains to be seen. On an evening like this you have to be on the lookout for opportunities. You never know what might go viral or who might give you a big media break. You have to watch and react quickly. That's my advice."

"Makes sense."

"Like the time when Jordanne Jacques started kissing Cindy Castellano at that gala to denounce heteronormativity. That was a stroke of genius."

"Um, yeah…"

"Don't make that face, Ellie. I'm not suggesting that we make out or anything."

"No, of course not. I know that!"

Oh dear God. I'm just too awkward. The truth is that all this is stressing me out more and more. Not just having to look perfect for the red carpet, but staging some big improvised media coup, just like that. I'm having a mini panic attack.

I don't know how Mila manages to always stay in control like this. Nothing rattles her. Next to her I look like an amateur.

"I could do your makeup for you if you want," she suggests.

"Okay, yes!"

Mila is very gentle with me. Maybe we're becoming real friends. At the same time, she would have every reason in the world to still blame me for what happened in our last year of high school.

THROWBACK

I only have a fairly vague memory of the last weeks of high school. I just remember that it was brutal. I didn't want to hear about any of the frenzied preparations for the formal. I wore my headphones at all times. I just couldn't stand listening to the girls in my class talk about how they'd been invited to prom.

All my hopes were dashed after François-Pierre Bouchard, my crush in final year, invited the drab, beige, insipid Cynthia Marcotte to go with him. He did it between two bites of a mustard and baloney sandwich in the cafeteria. Cynthia practically choked for joy on her apple-berry compote.

I know this because I was there. All of which is to say that I was not feeling it. Not at all, in fact.

Partly because things had become complicated between me and Mila.

Mila had taken to going to the art studio after class to work on her solo project. She was working on this gorgeous painting brimming with vibrant shades of yellow, orange, pink and green. It was a picture of a bird about to take off, symbolizing the end of adolescence, the passage into adulthood. It was a gigantic canvas that she was creating stroke by stroke with a palette knife.

It was a colossal work. A project far too ambitious for the time she had at her disposal. I'm not exaggerating when I say that everyone was holding their breath to see whether she would finish it on time.

Even unfinished, the canvas was so promising that it had already been selected for the front cover of the yearbook the following year.

As for me, things were not quite as glorious. I'd abandoned my sculpture depicting "the existential void," due to lack of inspiration (okay, lack of talent), and I'd fallen back on a mixed-media piece. My teacher had agreed to let me work on a new project, on the condition that I came to class at least two extra periods a week to catch up.

I'd decided to produce a series of portraits of my family done in dry pastel.

I wished it were something grander. That my ideas could result in something beautiful for once.

But my project, like all the others before it, was doomed to indifference and oblivion.

As I would find out soon enough.

26

The taxi drops us off in front of the performance hall. We could enter discreetly through the theater door like most people, but there's no question of going unnoticed. We came here to be seen.

Mila takes me by the hand and leads me towards the roped-off security at the entrance to the red carpet. A big gentleman in a suit with dark glasses and a tiny earpiece beckons us.

We're jubilant. It's just like in the movies.

I'm impressed by the number of photographers, journalists and attendants of all kinds who are busy around the stars.

I take a deep breath for courage and I make a happy face to Mila, who winks back at me.

"Let's do this, baby!"

We haven't taken two steps on the red carpet when a lady with a black cap, a stack of stapled sheets of paper and a walkie-talkie blocks our way to ask who we are and if we are on the list.

I stammer that I don't know. I give my name. She flips through her pages. Once. Twice.

I want to disappear.

All smiles, Mila walks over to talk to her discreetly. She says it might just be a mistake, because we are fairly well-known content creators.

The woman replies that the red carpet is reserved for artists and asks us to go directly through the door like all the invited media.

Mila loses nothing of her beautiful big smile and sneaks out her phone. She swivels on her heels and places her device directly in front of her to take a surprise selfie. The lady is far from impressed, but Mila leans very, very close to her face to tell her with a lot of velvet in her voice that half a million subscribers would be really disappointed to learn that an employee is being a bully on the red carpet of the anti-bullying concert.

I just keep smiling because of the photographers, but I seriously wonder if I'm being pranked. I feel really bad for the lady with the cap who after all is just doing her job.

I decide to turn back when I see Cap Lady, exasperated by Mila's attitude, waving us forward onto the carpet, as if to say good riddance.

More cheerful than ever, Mila waves. She even laughs loudly as she turns around, as if she's just had the most hilarious talk with her lifelong best friend.

I catch up with Mila, running like a penguin in my platform shoes. In front of the photographers, Mila poses. I do the same. I try to practice the little bits of advice she gave me in the taxi. To breathe, never stop smiling, stand up straight and imagine that everyone came just to see you.

We're stopped by a journalist from *Celebrity World*. Mila enthusiastically answers her questions. She looks like she's completely in her element. She floats on the red carpet like a star in the firmament.

As for me, I manage, but it takes every ounce of my energy. I don't know how I'm going to make it through the evening. It's exhausting.

After at least two thousand pictures of the two of us from one end of the red carpet to the other, I lean towards Mila to ask her THE question that I've been obsessing about ever since we got here.

"Did you know we weren't on the list?"

It makes her laugh.

While she waves to the crowd gathered in front of the theater to cheer on the stars, she replies, "First lesson, Ellie. If you want something, don't wait for someone to give it to you. Take it."

27

When we get into the hall, Mila heads for the bar. I trail behind her. In line, she keeps checking her phone. I ask whether she wants something to drink.

Without raising her eyes, she says, "Sparkling water with lemon. If I can give you a bit of advice, this is not the time to let your guard down."

"Uh, I had no intention of doing so."

Mila throws herself into the arms of a guy who has just tapped her on the shoulder.

It's Seb Hadiba, a YouTuber, Cath Bonenfant's ex.

He whispers something in Mila's ear, and she chuckles happily. She takes out her cell to make a story where you see her kissing Seb on the cheek over and over. Mila tags Seb, who will then immediately share it, too.

In the meantime, I get the two glasses of sparkling water I ordered, and Mila takes one.

"Come on. Seb has access to the VIP area."

I scan the room for familiar faces. I don't know anyone here. A super nice fan asks me to take a selfie with her, and I'm happy to say yes. Mila watches us in silence. We walk across the floor to another roped-off section that we get through with no problem. I get a little kick seeing all the well-known faces around me. There's Jordanne Jacques talking to the presenter Simon Ouellet. The whole cast from the series *High School*, a lot of old contestants from the reality show *Singles*, journalists and lots of content creators like us.

As much as I'm proud just to be one of them, I want to stand out, draw attention.

I make an extra effort to suck in my stomach and stand straight. I try to look intriguing and smart.

"Friendly tip," Mila whispers in my ear. "Make lots of new BFFs, and make sure you're part of as many stories as possible. It's the best promo, and it's free."

"Okay, sure."

"Looks like there's kombucha. Do you want some?"

I give her a thumbs up. She winks at me before heading for the VIP bar.

I'm starting to find Mila a bit patronizing with all her advice and friendly tips. I don't know whether she thinks I'm just a beginner at all this, but she's wrong. I feel like showing her she's underestimating me.

My heartbeat goes into third gear as I look around for someone to talk to. Mila herself is in the middle of a deep conversation with Seb Hadiba. I wonder whether they're sleeping together. I could go and join them to try to check it out, but I'd rather show Mila that I don't need her.

Two girls in matching cocktail dresses are taking selfies in front of the VIP section.

It's Emma and Juliette. They're twins. They've had a YouTube channel since they were teenagers. Two years ago they were at the top of the charts thanks to their reality show *The Life of Twins*. But tonight they look as though they're waiting for someone to let them in as Very Important People.

I know them. We collaborated back when I was getting started, but I hesitate. I'm not sure Mila would think it was a good idea to be seen with them. Given that they've made a few dubious choices recently. The comments on their Taylor Swift cover were brutal.

I gain some time by taking out my cell to text Sam. I send him three hearts and write "Thinking about you." I'd been planning to wait for him to send some news, but now that I'm alone in this crowd full of stars, writing to Sam is a real comfort.

I smile to look like I'm completely absorbed with

my phone, even though absolutely nothing is going on there.

Sam must already be on stage in Toronto.

I put away my phone and look up. The twins are leaning over the VIP rope and in deep conversation with Sophie Chen.

Sophie Chen. Now that would be a good place to start. Once she gets rid of the twins.

I sneak a glance at Mila. She's in the middle of taking a selfie with her glass of kombucha. One of her new BFFs, I imagine.

I burst out laughing and decide to go and say hi to Sophie even if I don't know her that well.

Sophie is a pretty basic influencer. She does unboxings, YouTube challenges that everyone's seen a hundred times and Day in My Life stuff where nothing at all happens. If you've watched a girl cook an egg while wearing yoga pants for four minutes, you've probably already seen a Sophie Chen video.

But hey, she's very nice, she dresses well, and she does have 300,000 followers.

I gently make my way around two or three people and head over to her. I give her two little taps on the shoulder.

She looks over, turning her back to the twins.

"Sophie!" I say. "Wow. Gorgeous outfit."

"Ellie! Hey, hello. Thanks. It's Gritzia from head to toe. Ha-ha!"

"You're sponsored? Fun!"

"Oh, no, but I can dream!" She raises her arms to the sky. "Gritzia, sponsor me, please! Ha-ha!"

I tell myself that it's unlikely Gritzia will sponsor someone with 300,000 subscribers, but I keep that thought to myself. Instead I give the twins a polite smile and wave at them over Sophie's shoulder.

Excited, Juju points at my shirt. "Is Samuel Vanasse with you? We'd love to get a photo with him for our Wall of Fame!"

Classic situation. I'm starting to get used to it. People who talk about my boyfriend before saying hello. It's annoying. Like I'm not a person in my own right.

Too bad for them. I plot a terrible revenge.

"Yes, but I haven't seen him for at least fifteen minutes. He may have gone out to get some air."

The twins exchange a hungry look, like the one my mother gives Nico at yoga. I shake off the image. They've obviously been waiting for just this moment.

Emma adjusts her bun and turns to me and Sophie.

"Ah, well, we're just going to go and freshen up before the show starts. Maybe we'll run into you later. See you!"

The twins pull up their strapless dresses in perfect sync and move towards the exit.

Sophie gives me a sympathetic finally-got-rid-of-them look. I get the message.

"Sam's in Toronto," I say, a bit proudly.

Sophie grabs two flutes of Champagne from a big round tray and hands one to me.

"Thank you so much. I thought they'd never leave."

"You're welcome."

"Party time!"

"Party time."

We clink glasses. I think about what would happen if I threw my glass right in her face. I wonder.

Sophie takes out her phone to immortalize our meeting in a story. A win for me, I tell myself.

At this moment the hall lights dim and Clara Fortier, the actor from *High School* and new spokesperson for the New Hope Foundation, comes on stage dressed in white. She's wearing a gown covered with feathers down the back, like the wings of an angel.

I find it a bit much and mention that to Sophie, who also thinks it's funny.

Looking solemn, Clara Fortier waits for the applause to die down. I'm already impatient for her to finish her little speech. I was just starting to have fun.

She finally starts to speak.

"We've gathered here this evening to talk about bullying. It is no longer a secret that I have been a victim myself. And something tells me that I am not the only one. I want to thank all the artists who have agreed to unite their voices to…"

I see Mila sitting at Jordanne Jacques' table. She looks over and her glance is icy. I can't help thinking about what happened at the final exhibition at high school. Is she thinking about it, too?

Does she still feel bad about it? Does she still blame me?

On stage, Clara Fortier continues.

"This must stop. We need to put an end to the shame and…"

I'm starting to feel unwell. I'm dizzy, and my hands are sweaty.

I look around for Mila. She's gone. Clara Fortier leaves the stage to applause. In front of me, a server is distributing glasses of wine. I grab a glass of white and take a few big gulps to take my mind off things. The lights go out and the room is plunged into darkness.

Clara Fortier's last words echo in my head. "We must stop being silent. Denounce them. Point a finger at the bullies among us."

There's an explosion of light on stage to signal the entrance of Coeur de pirate. The crowd goes wild as she starts to sing the first notes of "Crier tout bas."

That's when I get an idea. An idea that could be totally great or go really bad.

I don't know which one it will be yet.

THROWBACK

Two days before the graduate exhibition, I'm alone in the art room with Mila. We work without speaking to each other. It's after four-thirty. I've started a portrait of Alice in pastels while listening to my playlist of heartbreak songs. It's because of François-Pierre Bouchard, the guy who'd rather go to prom with that dry crust of toast Cynthia Marcotte.

I got off to a good start with my drawing, but I made the mistake in the positioning of the eyes and nose.

The result? Alice looks like a squinty-eyed sleazebag.

I'll have to start over. Exhibition day is almost here and so far I just have two decent drawings. For a second I imagine texting my sister to squint on the evening of the exhibition. My teacher wouldn't be able to tell the difference. Who knows, he might even be moved. Maybe give me a few bonus points?

No.

Discouraged, I look up at Mila. Perched on her stepladder, she applies a few touches of pink all over her canvas. Her strokes are delicate, precise, inspired.

I sigh. Through my headphones I hear the first notes of Radiohead's "Creep." It's the perfect soundtrack for my life as a girl failure.

"You're just like an angel..."

My eyes are still fixed on Mila. I tell myself I would give anything to be her just for one day, just for a single minute. To know what that's like.

I crumple up my paper, crush it into a small ball that I throw with all my strength into the recycling bin. The ball bounces off the back of a chair and rolls to land at the foot of Mila's ladder.

I sigh deeply. I can't even throw my own work in the garbage.

I get up to pick up my ball of paper and put it in the recycling bin.

At the same moment, Mila climbs down her ladder. Our eyes meet. Hers are filled with confetti. She has a little smile at the corner of her lips. She looks like a girl who floats like a feather in a beautiful world. So fuckin' special.

She puts down her palette knife to wipe her hands with a cloth before turning her canvas to the room to bring her creation to light.

I can't believe it. She finished it. She did it.

I watch her sign her canvas with black marker.

It's like I'm hypnotized. The result is amazing. It's the most beautiful thing I've ever seen in my entire life.

I feel the weight of gravity crush me to the ground as I return to my seat. It's like I'm stunned.

It's already almost five o'clock. Mila puts away her equipment quickly, takes a picture of her canvas and leaves without saying goodbye.

I jump up from my chair to lock the door behind her. I lower the blinds.

I want to be all alone with the painting. I want to look at it. For a long time.

"...*I wish I was special.*" Standing in front of Mila's work, the guitar chords make me shiver. My eyes wander over the art. They stroke the wings of the magnificent bird, slide into its colorful feathers and land on the signature "Mila Mongeau" in black marker at the bottom right.

Even her signature is beautiful. I linger there.

The M's of Mila and Mongeau...

I feel myself rocking...It starts slowly, a vague sensation, a tingling in my belly.

Then it's like an explosion. I stop breathing.

I recognize the M. The loop at the beginning, the rounded tops, the third leg longer than the others.

I recognize it because I've already seen it on a piece of paper I will never forget: "For Élisabeth. I'm sick of seeing your big ass in class. Time you tried getting into salad. MUCHO LOVE from everyone."

I feel an incredible sadness come over me. It's a familiar feeling. Strangely comforting.

I don't belong here.

I turn off the suave voice of Thom Yorke and cry a flood of tears. The failure of my life. My insignificance.

And I stay there, pathetically collapsed at the foot of the canvas by Mila Mongeau. That I love. That I hate.

28

It's 10:30 p.m. and I still can't find Mila.

I'm worried. The last time I saw her she was sitting at Jordanne Jacques' table. It was before the concert started. I went to find her after, but Sophie Chen pulled me into a small crowd in front of the stage to dance to "her" song.

After that we met up with her friend Charlie who was one of the volunteers. She got us a backstage pass and I saw the guys from Six Twenty-six, good friends of Sam. They made me do a few shots. They were disgusting, but I didn't dare refuse the first round. Or a second.

By the time I left there, I'd completely forgotten about Mila.

Until about two minutes ago when I went to her Instagram account to compare stories, and I realized that she hadn't posted anything since the kombucha.

That wasn't normal. I texted her, sent her a word on Messenger, a snap, a DM and I even tried to phone.

I'm going back to the VIP zone when I cross paths with Seb Hadiba and his gang, but no Mila. I go out to the front of the theater, where I have to tell the twins that Sam left before the start of the concert.

I look in the alley behind, go up to the balcony, take another selfie with fans, come back down, go to look in the washrooms.

I know she would never leave without me. Her apartment keys are in her suitcase, which is still on my bed.

I finally ask a guy whether he's seen a blonde girl in the men's washroom. He says no but that there are other washrooms upstairs.

Moving quickly now, I climb up to the balcony and finally find the bathroom in a dark corner at the end of a corridor.

As I push open the door, I suddenly think about coming across my mother and Nico in the middle of their damp and lazy lovemaking session. I realize that I still don't know how to handle that, though it will probably take the rest of my life. I laugh to myself.

No one in sight in the bathroom. My mind wanders while I fix my makeup in the mirror.

That's when I see Mila's sneakers under the door of a stall in the back.

"Phew!" I say, relieved. "I've been looking for you

everywhere! I thought something had happened to you."

"…"

"Are you okay?"

"Yeah."

I hear the noise of the toilet paper dispenser. While Mila finishes in there, I take the opportunity to touch up my lipstick and tell her about my evening.

"I've been chilling with Sophie Chen. She's cooler than I thought. What about you? Any stories? You'd be proud of me. I made lots of new BFFs backstage… Oh, yeah, and I have this brilliant idea!"

Mila opens the door of the stall. Her eyes are wet. Her nose is red. Her lipstick is smudged. Her mascara is running. She's tried to clean it up, but it's left blue marks under her eyes and on her eyelids.

Her arms crossed, she looks at me in the mirror.

I turn around.

"Shit! Are you okay?"

"Yes."

"What happened?"

"Nothing."

"Is it Seb Hadiba?"

"No."

"I'm sorry. I'm such a bad friend. I abandoned you all evening, and then —"

"I didn't need your help, Ellie. I'm a big girl."

She wipes the underside of her eyes to look at me closely.

"Have you been drinking?" she asks.

Surprised by her question, I make a big effort to look normal. "Well…a little."

"Looks like it. Be careful. This isn't really the place for that."

Mila washes her hands, then brushes a little water through her hair to smooth it down.

"So what's your brilliant idea."

"Oh…we can talk about it another time."

"No, I'm interested."

It's like she's challenging me. The timing isn't great, but I go ahead anyway.

"It might not be a good idea, but I thought we could tell our story. Publicly."

"What story?"

"Our story from high school."

Mila looks at me coldly. It's the first time I've raised the "incident" with her.

My voice is shaking, but I keep going. "It would be

incredible publicity for us. If you wanted a big boost, well, this is a dream opportunity. It would make a stunning video. Admit it!"

"No."

"No?"

"It's not a good idea."

"What? Hey, just think about it. It would attract sympathy from all sorts of people!"

"I don't think so. No."

"But it's a such a beautiful story. We were enemies, and now we're friends. It's beautiful because it's full of hope."

"We're not really friends, Élisabeth. I've told you that plenty of times. We are collaborating, that's all."

Mila's voice is calm and flat.

Suddenly I feel ridiculous.

"We'll share a taxi to your place," she says. "I'll fetch my suitcase, and then we'll go back to our lives like before, okay?"

I have a lump in my throat. I give a little nod.

"Pass me your lipstick, please," Mila says.

David Lanctôt has sent you a Facebook message

D: To never see each other again.

E: I admit that I miss having someone to hate wraps with.

D: That's what happens, huh? Once we start we can't stop. What are you doing that's good?

E: Well. I would say I'm not really doing much good at all. It's complicated. What about you?

D: That sucks. We can talk about it if you want.

E: Ah, no. That's nice of you, but it would take too long to explain. What's going on with you?

D: OK, well, call me if you change your mind. I'm not really sleeping.

D: I'd love to hear your voice.

CELEBRITY WORLD

Jordanne Jacques has found love again!

Influencer Jordanne Jacques, who went through a very difficult (and very public) breakup with her ex Marine Lorrain, can now turn the page because this beauty has found love in the arms of YouTuber Seb Hadiba (that's right, Cath Bonenfant's ex). We wish them lots of happiness and we'll keep our fingers crossed because . . .

Fantastic red carpet at the gala against bullying [photos]

The stars looked beautiful on the red carpet at the magnificent annual benefit concert for the New Hope Foundation, which fights against bullying in schools. The electrifying evening was packed with celebrities and raised the impressive sum of . . .

Ellie of Quinoa Forever and Mila Mongeau were friends in high school!

On Instagram we learned that Ellie Bourdon-Marois and Mila Mongeau were good friends in high school. After losing touch with each other for several years, they've revived their friendship thanks to their jobs as influencers. To our delight, the two web stars have announced that they are collaborating on a new video series. We can't wait to see . . .

29

11:15 p.m. Mila and I didn't exchange a word during the whole taxi ride. She was on her cell, and so was I.

I pay the driver, and we go up.

She takes her suitcase off my bed.

"Big party," she says.

"Yeah…"

Endless silence. It's like she's trying to apologize but doesn't know how.

I breathe in and out gently to give her some space. Reduce the tension.

Finally, she says, "Drink hot water with lemon. It's good for the day after…"

"Sure. I'll be okay."

I lock the door behind Mila and crash onto my couch. I feel completely messed up, but it's not the alcohol. I've been sober for a long time.

No, I realize that I haven't eaten anything all evening. I've eaten nothing, but I've ingested at least six hundred liquid calories.

Seriously, what was I thinking? This is really not the time. I should be able to control my dietary intake better than this. I wrote a book about it, for Christ's sake.

Tomorrow I'm back to being hard-core. No sugar, no carbs, a ton of vegetables and working out every day. Cardio and strength training.

I'm getting up to get a healthy snack from the kitchen when I realize that Sam never responded to my text at the beginning of the evening.

I check my cell. Nope. I open Messenger. I see that he was "active 42 minutes ago."

He must have just forgotten, I tell myself.

"How was your concert," I write. "Things aren't feeling that great here. Send news. I miss you. XXX."

I make myself a rice cake with hummus. I go back to the living room to eat it. I return to the kitchen, pour a glass of water.

I look at my cell. Nothing. I turn on the ringer. I put on the kettle to make a herbal tea. While I wait for it to boil, I nibble on half a rice cake. I cut myself a piece of cheese that I swallow in one bite.

It's cold, it's salty. I want more.

I eat some baby carrots instead and go back to the living room. I take my laptop, bite into a carrot. Look for photos of the red carpet.

I find them. Sigh. Beside Mila, I look like a tuna fish.

I close the page. Open my email which informs

me about a sale at Gritzia. Chew on another carrot. I click on a buttoned black dress in merino wool. I waver between two sizes.

In the kitchen, I hear the water boiling. Chew on a carrot.

I end up telling myself that it would be better to wait until I get back to my "ideal weight" before buying new clothes.

I look at the bag of carrots. Meh. The kettle whistle gets louder and louder.

I get up. I turn off the stove. I pour myself a cup of boiling water and add two tea bags — one Sleepy Dreams and one Citrus Slim. This is no time to fool around.

I look at my cell. Still nothing. I rummage around the pantry. I want something sweet. Just a taste.

Sam bought cookies. Chocolate chip and strawberry jam.

Strawberry, that's a fruit.

I take a cookie. I close the box back up immediately so I won't eat two of them.

I get a text. It's my mother. She wants to talk tomorrow.

Shit, I ate while I was reading. I ruined my cookie

moment. The sugary sweetness lingers in my mouth.

I bargain with myself for one last cookie.

Deal. I eat it. I go to put back the box and realize I have not tasted the chocolate chip ones.

Whatever, I'll try one. Just one. It's just for a taste.

I close the box back up. I force myself to eat it slowly. To enjoy it.

It's so good. I want more. I realize that I've eaten three cookies and cheese. Three cookies, cheese and at least six hundred calories of alcohol. That's almost one thousand calories not counting the rice crackers.

I've messed up again. I tell myself fuck that.

Tomorrow I'll start to eat well. Tomorrow I'll pull myself together.

There, this is too good to stop. I reopen the box of chocolate chip cookies. I eat one. I eat two. I eat three. I eat four. I eat five. I eat six. I eat seven. I eat eight. I eat nine. I eat ten.

I stop counting. For a minute I'm floating.

Coming back to earth is brutal. I grab the box of cookies. I go out to the back balcony. I take the fire escape stairs down to my neighbor's. I open her recycle bin and stuff in Sam's empty chocolate chip cookie box.

I sneak back upstairs. I throw the crumbs in the garbage. I swallow my tea. I brush my teeth. I drink water. I have a stomachache.

The worst thing is that I see my coach tomorrow. She's going to weigh me. I hate myself.

I set my alarm for 6:45 a.m. so I can do a big workout. A double workout. I go over the list of exercises I'm going to do in my head. I am motivated for two seconds.

Then I tell myself it won't do any good. I tell myself that I have already ruined everything. I blame myself for the cookies. I tell myself that I should sleep.

I can't sleep.

I open Messenger. I reread the message from Dave.

I click on his number and press Call.

It rings twice.

"David Lanctôt speaking."

"Oh my God, you answer the phone just like my father!"

Text messages between Estelle and Ellie

Estelle: Sweetheart, I would like to have a quick chat. Will you come for dinner tomorrow?

Ellie: Well . . . can we talk at yoga this week? I already have a big day today.

Estelle: No, it can't wait. I can come to you. Wherever suits you.

Ellie: Okay . . . Café B, corner of Laurier and St-André. 1 p.m.?

Estelle: Okay. We'll talk about your Christmas recipes too.

Ellie: Good idea!

Samuel Vanasse has sent you a Facebook message

S: Sorry, I lost my charger. We are ON FIRE here. I'll try to FaceTime you from the road sometime. X

30

It's never too late to be what you might have been.

This is what is written on my coach Josiane's 1.5-liter isothermal rose-gold water bottle with integrated straw lid.

As I walk into her office, I take off my shoes, my socks and my sweater. Without saying a word, I climb on the DeepBÖDY machine to weigh myself. I place my feet on the sensors. They're cold. I grab the little metal handles, one in each hand.

While Josiane starts the analysis by pressing a lot of small buttons, I silently pray for a miracle. I lengthen my neck and try to send my weight up into the air, as if I'm about to fly away.

At the end of a few dozen seconds, I hear two long beeps, the signal for me to let go of the handles, get down and put my socks back on.

I've always found it embarrassing, putting on my socks in front of someone. Dressing my feet. It makes me feel like a child.

Josiane takes my results out of the printer and sits down at her desk on a big exercise ball that she uses as a chair. She circles numbers with her pink marker — percentage of fat, muscle mass, detailed composition of my torso, my arms, my legs and my level of hydration.

Then, bouncing lightly on her ball, she wrinkles her eyebrows. She looks at me with an enigmatic smile, opens my file and takes out the results of my last two tests for comparison.

It's almost unbearable to watch her discover what I already know. I'm visibly getting bigger.

"How is the training going for the half marathon?"

"Good at first, but at some point…it was starting to piss me off. So I quit."

Josiane recoils a bit on her ball. She's not used to hearing me talk like this. Neither am I, but it just came out.

"Did you injure yourself?" she asks. "Have you been following the plan precisely? Often new runners hurt themselves when they try to start out too fast. Do you want to —"

"No, it's not that. I was following the plan, but at some point I realized that you just have to keep running for longer, farther, faster and —"

"We can adjust the —"

"But you never get anywhere. You run, you run,

you give it everything you have, but you never arrive anywhere."

Josiane looks at me, puzzled. I keep talking, transported by my own words like I'm some great NASA scientist reflecting out loud on the phenomenon of black holes.

"Then you start all over again. Your best time yesterday is worth nothing if you can't do it again today. It's all about starting over again and you never get anywhere."

"..."

"Ever."

"But that's the fun, Ellie! To keep getting better day after day!"

I don't reply. Josiane gives me a big worried smile.

"I think I'm tired," I say.

"Of course! Because you're also dehydrated! And a girl who's dehydrated is what?"

"I don't know."

"It's a girl who is de..."

"...dehumidified?"

"...DEMOTIVATED!"

BODY POSITIVE

I see more and more fat girls posing naked on Instagram. Girls with bodies that don't fit into conventional standards and who aren't trying to change that. Who aren't trying to lose weight. Who refuse to be the Before for the Afters. Who have the courage to be fat in a world that hates fat people.

When I see these girls on the front lines showing off their bellies and their thighs, I tell myself that this is real courage. That real courage is not "taking charge." It's to stop trying to do so. It's accepting that you're not going to fit in.

I know I won't make any friends by saying this, but those super slim Instagrammers #legdayeveryday who say they are #bodypositive? I find them hypocritical as fuck. I don't think they realize it. I guess it all starts with good intentions, but I think...by what right? By what right do you appropriate someone else's struggle? As if you too are out there with your body on the front lines. As if you're accepting it for what it is. I mean, how can you seriously say to yourself that you're for the acceptance of all bodies, when you spend your time trying to fit yours into the mold?

Hey, I'm not saying that I accept my body, but at least I'm not pretending that I do. I spend two-thirds of my life getting my body under control. My whole life is organized around this. And I admit that it pisses me off seeing posts from girls in super tight leggings flashing their tight round butts and their tiny waists as thin as my little finger, and reading under their posts stuff like *Love, please know that you have always been enough #bodypositive #selfconfidence #selflove #bliss.* I'd like to take these Instagrammers by the scruff of their hoodies and ask them, "Do you see everything you do in a day just to feel good? Just to deserve the right to exist? Do you see that we're all caught on this same damn treadmill that's crushing us with its diets and two hundred bucks at Glamora? That before you can be a woman you're still just a body?"

Don't give me that *This is bliss* bullshit.

No, but there are a lot of girls who don't feel like they're "enough," and I wish we would stop telling them it's all in their heads. That they're just making it up.

The world isn't made for us to feel like we're good enough the way we are, okay?

We have to stop saying that our weight and our

appearance are a matter of personal choice. That it's a matter of willpower and self-love. Bullshit! Stop it already! If we stopped saying one thing and then doing exactly the opposite, that would be a start.

No girl finds it easy to love her body. Not a single one of us. And I'd love it if someone would prove me wrong.

But... I mean... at least I'm not pretending. At least I'm not a hypocrite like the others.

Right?

31

I walk into Café B determined to play the role of my life. An Oscar-worthy performance, I hope, with me playing the part of a girl who, completely by chance, is meeting her mother in a café owned by a guy she talked to on the phone for forty minutes last night.

The truth, of course, is that I want to see Dave. I think about him. Way too often. My theory is that I need to spend a bit more time with him, and then I'll be able to put it all behind me. Otherwise it will keep being too special, and I'll keep idealizing him.

If I'm around him a little, I'll see that he's just ordinary.

At least, that's the new game plan.

I scan the room, ready to meet his gaze. Ready to melt secretly when he smiles at me.

But he's not here. I say hello to my mother while I continue to look around the room.

She grabs her latte to take to the counter.

"I only have five minutes," she says. "I have to see my acupuncturist at one thirty."

It's perfect. I was afraid she would embarrass me in front of Dave. Or, worse, that she might guess that

I have . . . a little crush on him.

On the other hand, if she leaves too quickly, there goes my alibi.

Nothing's ever easy.

"What did you want to talk about?" I ask.

My mother throws her sunglasses on the table close to the counter before sitting on the edge of a chair. I take off my jean jacket. She keeps on her coat and her shoulder bag. I sit down facing her, curious.

I hope it's nothing serious. Early-onset Alzheimer's or worse.

"Well, sweetie, as you surely have noticed, I have a new partner."

"A partner?"

"Yes."

Partner. Such a ridiculous term. Sounds like a business merger.

"Oh, wow. I'm happy for you!"

"Don't you want to know who it is?"

"Sure . . . do I know him?"

"It's Nicolas."

". . ."

". . ."

"Nico?"

"Nico."

"Yoga Nico?"

Breathe-into-your-back Nico. Contract-your-pelvic-floor Nico.

Nico, my mother's... partner.

I don't believe it! I mean, it's too much. My mother needs me to explain a few things to her before it's too late.

"Maman, having a... fling with a younger man is one thing. But, a partner? He's what, twenty-five? I don't think he's looking to be your partner. Okay? These days just because you... with someone it doesn't mean they automatically become your partner. Do you understand what I'm saying?"

"Absolutely. Do you think this is my first walk around the block, Élisabeth? You know I've known several men, both before and after your father."

"Agh, Maman! Don't say 'I've known men' like that. Just... don't. No."

"What, you'd prefer that I say I fucked several men?"

"No, stop it!"

"Élisabeth, you're acting like a teenager."

"Okay, whatever. Does Nico know that he's your... partner?"

"To be frank, Nicolas is in love with me. Is that so difficult to imagine?"

"No...no. I'm asking because..."

I'm on slippery ground here. I decide not to finish my sentence. Instead I make a strategic retreat and make a vague gesture with my arms. Then I let out a big sigh.

"Because...nothing. I didn't say anything."

"I admit that I might have expected this reaction from Alice, but I'm a bit disappointed to see it from you, Élisabeth. We've fallen in love and that's all there is to it. We didn't choose this! Do you think I wanted to fall in love with Nico? No. But there it is. As they say, 'The heart has its reasons, whereof reason knows nothing.'"

"I understand."

Not. That theory about how we fall in love? That we don't choose it? I don't believe it for two seconds. There is a moment when we choose to fall in love. There's always a moment when you can decide to stop, to get out, or to stay and let yourself fall.

But I'm not going to get into this with my mother, obviously.

"Really, I'm happy for you, Maman."

"So, I can count on you to...You know where I'm going with this. I'd like you to help me tell Alice. You know your sister. Nicolas has been the first man since your father to be 'officially' in my life. I'm afraid this will throw her. That and..."

It's my mother's turn to be at a loss for words. I know exactly what she's thinking, but I wait for her to say it out loud.

"And what?"

"The age difference."

"Well, yeah! Um...How many years are we talking about, exactly?"

"Forty-nine minus twenty-eight, that makes — what? About twenty."

"Twenty-one."

"Twenty-one. If you say so."

My mother is looking at her hands. She's pretending to examine the state of her manicure. I think I've hurt her feelings. I feel bad. It's even moving to see my mother in this impossible grand love story. I can see in her eyes that she's having the trip of her life. And no doubt coming down from it will be brutal when Nico leaves her for someone in their twenties. I figure it will take three weeks, but I hope she can really enjoy it until then.

"Okay. I'll talk to Alice."

I know my sister. It's better for me to be the one who tells her. I haven't talked to her since the dinner with my father. We need to make up soon. I'm still a bit pissed, but I really need her to show up for my Karma Christmas photo shoot. The sponsor wants family photos.

My mother gets up to leave the café. As if she's reading my thoughts, she says, "Oh, and you can count on one more guest for your Karma Christmas dinner. Blended families, that's the new normal anyway."

Just what I need. I stop myself from telling my mother that people are going to think Nico is Alice's boyfriend. One thing at a time.

"I'm off. Hugs, sweetie!"

"Hugs to you."

I watch my mother leave. Wearing her expensive jeans. Her freshly styled hair. Her slightly superior attitude.

I feel a combination of sadness and love for her. I want to text her a nice little note. A heart. I never tell her I love her when she's actually there.

My little maman.

32

"I'm glad you came, Quinoa, because I have a few questions."

I turn to see who's talking behind me.

It's Dave. My heart silently explodes, I'm so happy to see him.

He is standing tall, his eyes sparkling, a dishcloth over his shoulder, a mug in his hand.

He's shaved off his beard and he's growing a moustache. I'm not sure how I feel about it yet.

"What? You've been here the whole time?"

Dave sits down facing me and signals one of his staff to bring us coffees. I ask for green tea.

He raises his eyebrows. Making him react is quickly becoming my favorite pastime.

Dave takes out his cell, opens his Notes application and says, "I took a look at your Instagram account last night. I need you to explain a few things to me."

"You made a list of questions? For real?"

"Yes. You have a couple of minutes to spare, I hope?"

I melt at the thought that Dave was stalking me after we talked on the phone.

"Sure. Shoot."

"First question: Does yogurt make you laugh?"

"What?!" I wrinkle up my nose and eyebrows. "What are you talking about, David Lanctôt?"

Dave shows me photos of myself taken for a campaign with Yaourti. In one, I'm sitting astride a giant inflatable flamingo in the middle of a gorgeous swimming pool and laughing while I eat a Yaourti watermelon yogurt. In the other I'm wearing a wide-brimmed hat and having a picnic at the end of a dock overlooking a magnificent lake. I'm holding a grapefruit Yaourti in one hand, a spoon in the other, and I'm laughing with joy as I gaze out at the horizon.

"Wait," he says. "There are others."

"That's okay. Stop. I confess! I wasn't really laughing. It was staged. Not only that, but it was super cold out."

"So?"

"So, no. Yogurt does not make me laugh. But the watermelon flavor is really good."

Satisfied, Dave returns to his list.

"So, 'Does not make her laugh.' Check. Okay, between us, do you really eat vegetables for breakfast?"

He shows me one of my posts where I am eating

scrambled eggs with spinach, kale and broccoli for breakfast.

"For real, yes. Often. They're loaded with vitamins! What better way to start the day than with vitamins?"

"Nope. Next question. Who takes these photos? Take this one where you're in your pajamas in your kitchen, glued to this charming young man named…"

"Sam."

"Sam! So, there's a third person who is taking the photographs while you are glued together wearing your fancy slippers, is that it?"

"Yes."

"Who is it?"

"Bianca Desmarais, a professional photographer."

"Oh shit. Is she here right now? Hiding in the bushes? Ready to immortalize your next autumnal latte moment wearing an extra-large woolen scarf?"

"No!"

I know Dave is making fun of me big time, but I like it.

"Tell the truth, Quinoa. Are there really numerous people out there wondering about your skin care routine?"

I know what he's referring to. A recent photo of me with an avocado beauty mask where I announce the launch of my beauty routine video. The caption under the photo says, "A number of you have been asking me about my skin care routine...blah, blah."

Proud that he can't catch me out on that one, I say, "Honestly, yes!"

"But no! It's impossible. How? In what context? Like, hello, how are you and by the way can you talk to me about your skin care routine?"

"In private messages or in the comments. People want to know which products I use. I swear!"

"Amazing."

Dave plunges back into his list of questions but raises his head immediately.

"When you say 'a number of you,' about how many people are you talking about? Just to give me an idea."

Shit. Touché. This is too much for me. I raise my eyes to the heavens, then smile widely before making the disturbing confession.

"Well...at least three or four."

"Wow. Three or four!"

I'm embarrassed to admit that, but I still burst out laughing because it is just too funny.

Thinking it over, I add, "Maybe even just two."

"Two! Unbelievable."

"So what. They have the right to know!"

Dave is in stitches. Me, too. We keep laughing for a good minute. It's so funny that my stomach hurts.

"Two. Two! Two people!"

I have to wipe the corners of my eyes because I am crying with laughter.

Dave takes a big sip of coffee before continuing with the next question.

"Okay, okay. Last one, I promise. Do I still have the chance to win a package of housewares worth $300 if I tag 'a friend who likes shiny things?'"

"The contest is over, sorry."

"Damn!"

I stare into his eyes. I wonder whether he notices that I'm looking at him a little more intensely than usual. Whether that does anything for him.

"Your mustache is cute," I say.

I don't know if I'm imagining it, but I think he's blushing.

"So," I say, satisfied. "Have you finished laughing at me?"

My eyes slide down. I have to concentrate on not

looking at his mouth. His lips. That would be...

No.

"I'm not laughing at you," he says.

"Well, maybe just a little."

"I admit it. It's because I really like you, Quinoa."

"Since when do you call me Quinoa? Stop it right now."

"Ellie. I really like you, Ellie."

Listening to those words coming out of Dave's mouth makes something capsize inside me.

Suddenly I don't feel in control of myself. I want to grab him by the neck and kiss him. I want to see him naked. To eat breakfast with him.

I try to get hold of my thoughts but I can't. I'm flailing around for a solution. Some explanation.

I think about Denise at the pharmacy. Her thing about listening to the little voice. I ask myself what she would say at this moment, my inner Denise...

Probably something like, "Run, Ellie. Run. Go home and do some burpees to calm yourself down."

Ah, no, but that's not what she's saying.

Everything is great, she says.

Everything is great. Holy shit. My inner voice is speaking to me. It's talking. And I realize that everything is great. That I feel good. I feel good.

I bite the inside of my cheek to make sure I'm not dreaming or anything.

No, I really feel good. That's it, I think, and I decide not to stop it. I decide that I need this guy in my life. That I have no idea how I'm going to manage it, or what the consequences will be, but at this moment, I don't care.

"Great. I have to go," Dave says. "Work calls."

"Okay, sure. Bye!"

"There's a party at your sister's place tonight. Are you going?"

I had no idea, but I pretend that I knew all about it.

"Uh...maybe. I haven't decided yet. Are you?"

"I think so. If you're going to be there."

Dave winks at me, blows me a kiss, grabs his mug and goes back to the kitchen.

I gather up my things. I look at the small ring of coffee his cup left on the table.

He's just left, and I miss him already.

Text messages between Ellie and Alice

E: Baby sister, what are you doing tonight? We should talk. It's important.

A: Karaoke night at the apartment for Opale's birthday.

E: What time? Can I come round a little early? It really won't take long.

A: Yep. Around 9-ish. Come any time after 7:30. We're ordering in Thai.

33

8:40 p.m. I knock on the door of Alice's apartment.
I have it all planned out. The plan is to try to make
peace over the other situation with Papa, providing
Alice takes some responsibility for it, then tell her
about Maman's boyfriend.

If that goes well, she'll invite me to stay for the
party. If it goes badly, I'll try to hang on until at least
9:15 p.m. in the hopes of running into Dave.

Apart from that, we'll see. I can't predict what will
happen.

It's Opale who opens the door. She's wearing a
shiny party hat, a Birthday Girl button and a big
necklace of fake pink pearls.

"Hi, I'm here to see Alice. I won't stay long."

"Fun."

In spite of her festive accessories, Opale seems to
be in a bad mood.

Impressive. It is her official superpower.

"Happy birthday, by the way," I say.

I follow her down the hall to the kitchen. When
she walks, Opale drags her feet on the floor. Kind
of like she has very small knees or gigantic heels. It

would annoy my mother a lot, this kind of walk. She always insists that my sister and I pick up our feet.

When I go into the kitchen, I recognize her roommate Maya, Arnaud the soft-cushion guy, and two other girls I've already met at Alice's.

My sister is sitting on the counter. She laughs as she reads aloud her fortune from her fortune cookie.

"You are going to get new clothes."

"Great news!" I say loudly without thinking. Everyone laughs. Even Alice, who grabs her glass of red and invites me to follow her to her room.

With her free hand, she sweeps a huge pile of laundry off her bed and then sits down. I sit in her desk chair, like I'm being punished.

She takes a big swallow of red.

"So?" she asks. "What's going on?"

I launch right in, trying to sound convincing.

"Well, I wanted to talk about the other day, with Papa."

"Yeah ... I'm really sorry about that, Ellie. Seriously. I've been thinking it over, and you're right. I went too far. And you felt bad and, well, it really isn't fair for me to put you in that position. I'm sorry."

I was expecting Alice to defend herself a bit more

vigorously than that. It's almost fishy.

Anyway, so much the better. First step of my plan. Check.

"Apology accepted. I'm sorry, too. I shouldn't have said what I said about you and Jeff. I don't know where that came from. Sometimes I get very emotional, and I lose control —"

"Ellie, are you serious? You think I'm mad about that?"

"Well...a little. Just a bit, no?"

"Absolutely not! On the contrary, you were right!"

Alice grabs a pillow, slides it behind her head and lies back before continuing. She speaks to the cciling.

"At first I was in complete denial. But at the same time, I wasn't able to stop thinking about what you said. Then I finally realized that it was true! I went into soc to please Jeff. Hundred percent!"

Alice digs behind her back. She squirms and pulls on the leg of a Little Mermaid pajama bottom, which she then tosses into a corner of her room.

"So once I understood that, I really thought about it. It looks like pretty much everything I've done in my life so far has been to please some guy. Not always the same one, of course...it's just that I realize I'm always looking for male approval. You might say it's the only thing that motivates me, you know what I mean?"

"Maybe a bit, but I think —"

"You know, it's unbelievable how many examples I have! In high school, I learned how to play the guitar because I had a crush on Ben. I went vegetarian to get closer to Simon. I went into Arts and Letters at CEGEP because I knew it would make Papa happy. Afterwards, I studied philosophy to be with Guillermo. I took a law course to try to impress Marc-Alexandre. I went backpacking around Europe just to have an excuse to go to London to see Antoine. Which is where I met Jeff, a sociology prof, and then two months later I'm signing up for a soc degree. Hello! It's so obvious that I have this pattern."

"When you say it like that, I guess —"

"Like, I realize I don't know myself at all. It's wild that I'm twenty-three years old and have no idea what I really want in life. About who I am when I'm not trying to please someone else, you know?"

I wasn't expecting this. I almost feel like Alice is having me on, but no, she seems completely sincere with this bolt of self-awareness.

I'm not sure what to say.

"Wow...that's...huge!"

"That's why I've decided to...No, wait, come on!"

Alice swallows the rest of her wine, leaves her glass on the floor and drags me by the wrist to the kitchen, where a small group of guests surround Opale and Maya.

Alice grabs a bottle of gin from the counter, chopsticks from the table and then climbs up onto a chair.

"Your attention, please!"

She taps the chopsticks on the gin bottle, but it doesn't make any noise. She decides to talk very, very loudly instead.

"Hey! I have a big announcement to make!"

Everyone turns towards Alice, who pretends to clear her throat.

"Ladies and gentlemen, I am announcing that as of today, I am embarking on a year-long sabbatical from SEX!"

As if she has been touched by heaven, Alice spreads her arms in the air, to the quiet applause of her friends.

Maya spits her mouthful of red wine into her glass and shouts, "Sabbatical from sex?!"

Alice unscrews the cap from the gin bottle, lifts it in a toast and takes a big swig before answering, "That's right. No sex, girl! No sexualidad!"

Alice gets down from her chair and leaps over to give me a hug.

"Thank you, Ellie. You are the best big sister. And I'm sorry again."

She grabs my shoulders and asks, "But you came to tell me something important?"

Geez, things are going too well. No way that I'm going to tell her about Maman's new "partner" or even the Christmas photo shoot right now.

"Ah, it's nothing," I say, taking the bottle from her hands. "I just wanted to clarify things. And I wanted to spend time with you."

I take a big swallow of gin right in Alice's astonished face, and she stamps her foot with joy.

"Great stuff! Stay for the party!"

"Hmmm, well…. okay!"

Drinking gin without any tonic? It's like brushing your teeth without toothpaste.

It's disgusting.

34

9:30 p.m. My hands are sweating. My heart races each time the apartment door opens. Holding onto my glass, I wait impatiently for Dave, leaning against the door frame between the corridor and the living room.

I look ridiculous, even to myself.

I've been thinking about Dave since this morning. Okay, since yesterday evening.

Okay, longer than that.

Contrary to what you might think, I'm not planning to cheat on my boyfriend or whatever. I just want to be with Dave, breathe in his smell, listen to him talking to me. Because it makes me feel good. That's all.

Anyway, Sam is so involved in his concerts, he hasn't even replied to my messages or anything. I can have a nice evening, too. It's not like we're going to make out. Honestly.

In the living room, Alice starts the karaoke machine to the cheers of her friends. She's picked "Africa" by Toto in a duet with Opale.

I know enough about karaoke to know it's a big

mistake. "Africa" seems like a pretty easy song to sing, but the chorus is awfully high-pitched.

It's too late to warn Alice…She's holding the microphone in one hand with her other arm around Opale.

Maya joins in with way too much enthusiasm. Poor thing, if she only knew what was coming. Still, I think they're beautiful, the three of them together. I don't think I've ever been as close to someone as Alice is to her roommates. She's lucky.

Uh-oh, here comes the chorus in three, two, one…

"I bless the rains down in Africa…" As expected, Alice, Opale and Maya do not manage to stay in tune. Which causes a thunder of laughter and applause in the room.

Just as well, because they spend a good four minutes shouting themselves hoarse like that.

I'm not saying this to be cool, but I think that if I could give out one piece of life advice, it would be this. Find two songs that you can sing for karaoke and then stick to them. Unless you're maybe Céline Dion. In which case you have to sing "My Heart Will Go On." Over and over and over.

In the living room, Opale throws in the towel as Alice and Maya courageously carry on.

I'm pulled from my thoughts by a warm and familiar voice when I hear someone behind me say, "'Africa.' Big mistake."

I don't even have to turn around, I know it's Dave. His presence behind my back warms me.

I smile without looking back.

"Good to see you, Quinoa," Dave whispers in my ear. His cheek brushes my hair. His chest brushes my shoulder. I shiver.

Dave plunges his eyes into mine. I immediately understand that we're not going to be debating the spelling of the word pretzel. Not tonight.

Dave smiles at me. I feel like he can see right inside me.

"I missed you," I say.

"I hope so," he replies.

At karaoke, Arnaud begins the first verse of "Harvest Moon" by Neil Young.

Excellent choice, I say to myself without taking my eyes off Dave. He takes me by the waist and leads me to the living room. I guess it's an invitation to dance. I look around to make sure no one's paying attention to us.

The living room is packed. My sister is dancing

with Opale. Maya is looking for a song on her cell. All's clear.

I snuggle into Dave's arms like we've come home.

He holds me close. I press my cheek to his. I think of nothing else but the weight of his hands on my hips. The meeting of our bodies.

I close my eyes.

I hold on to every second I spend in his arms. I want them to last forever.

"We could dream this night away…"

"We can't stay here."

"Follow me," Dave says, taking my hand.

The air I'm breathing becomes fizzy. While Arnaud sings the last verse in the living room, we go down the hall to Alice's room.

Without taking his eyes off me, Dave sits on the bed. I stay standing, leaning against the door to look at him. I want to kiss him, but I stay there, my lips half parted to wait to see what he'll do.

Dave deliberately draws out the moment. He looks at me. Touches every part of my body with his eyes.

I'm about to dissolve in the air. He stands up, reaches out, grabs my hips and pulls me to him.

I sigh with relief. He slides his hand up to my neck. Puts his lips on mine, caresses them with his mouth. I plunge my tongue into his mouth.

It is just what I'd hoped. It is perfect. I'm flying.

Dave gently takes my wrist, lifts my arm above my head and presses me against the door. I feel myself melt. I kiss his cheek. The skin of his neck. I bite him. He pushes me back onto the bed. Our mouths meet. I grab onto his back with my legs. I want to feel him against me. I want…

But he pulls away. His eyes look worried. My heart is racing.

"Just reassure me, Ellie," he says.

"What?"

"That this is no mouth accident?"

"You are such an asshole, David Lanctôt."

Satisfied, Dave kisses me again and again, and I slowly come to realize what I am about to do. Lying on Alice's bed. My hands thrust under Dave's sweater. Wrapped up in him.

This wasn't the plan.

I tell myself, just another minute. One more minute and I'll quit. One last minute, just one minute…

And I take advantage of every second.

Then I push Dave away gently.

"I can't…keep going. Even though I want to."

He lies beside me. I snuggle up against him, his chest against my back.

After a minute or two, he asks, "So when was it… when you fell for me?"

I laugh. It's a cute question. I take my time thinking about it.

"The hug in front of the Metro. No! Before that, I admit it. Argh. If I'm really honest, I think it was when you came back to say goodbye at Alice's party."

"When you pushed me into the coats, you mean!"

Dave brings his hand to my face. His palm scratches my nose a bit. He gently bats my head from side to side. It makes me laugh. I take his hand and kiss it.

"Just before," I say.

"…"

"What about you?"

"As soon as I saw you."

"That's cheating."

"No, it's true."

"Okay, what did you say to yourself when you saw me?"

"That I couldn't let you go."

"Meh."

"I swear it's true."

35

10:40 p.m. What had to happen happens.

Alice comes into her room to top up her deodorant. She finds us, Dave and me, snuggled up together. In her bed, to boot.

I just hope it isn't as traumatic for her as the time I surprised my mother and Nico at yoga.

I jump out of bed. Dave gets up, too.

He looks deep into my eyes to try to gauge how I'm feeling. Says he's going to leave us sisters to sort things out.

I don't want him to go, but at the same time, I don't see how it can be any other way.

"Okay," I say. "That's probably a good idea."

Ideas are bouncing around in my head. I just cannot imagine how I'm going to go back to my normal life after this.

Dave gives me one last hug and whispers, "Let me know how it goes, Quinoa."

I watch him go, half delighted, half devastated at the thought of what's just happened.

I must have quite the look on my face, because Alice asks me sarcastically, "Do you want to talk about it?"

"You have no idea!"

"Okay, but I'm dying of hunger. We can debrief over poutine. My treat."

36

11:00 p.m. I sit on one of the benches at the back of Chez Ma Tante while Alice puts in our order at the counter. She puts two bottles of beer on the table and sits down across from me. Excited, she bangs her Porter 50 against my Buck light and instructs me to tell her everything.

"What the what, Ellie? I think I'm missing something."

I tell her the whole story of what's happened since her birthday. The incredible chemistry. The accidental kiss. The surprise meetings. The messages. The middle-of-the-night phone call. My visit to the café. The invitation to Opale's party. The non-accidental kisses.

All of it.

Alice listens as attentively as if I were telling her how I was going to solve the global warming crisis. The server brings us a plate overflowing with poutine, green peas and bacon. I realize that I haven't eaten anything since noon. I dig in.

With her mouth full, she throws out the killer question.

"Are you in love?"

"Aagh, fuck off, Alice Bourdon-Marois! Don't ask me that! It's not nice."

"Why not?"

"Because...I already have a boyfriend...I can't just be in love with someone else...It's not that simple."

"Okay. Are you in love with Sam, to start? Really in love? Not like, 'Teehee, it's Samuel Vanasse, and I'm super thrilled that he's into me, since I'm nothing without all those likes and everyone else's approval.'"

"That's just mean, Alice."

"No, admit it."

"..."

"Have you ever been in love with Sam? Honestly?"

"You are the absolute worst!"

The terrible thing about all this is that deep inside, I know that she's got a point. That what I feel for Sam isn't...It's like Dave has made me discover feelings that I didn't know existed. But it's going too fast. I'm all confused.

"Yes. I do love Sam. It's different, okay, but that doesn't mean it's less —"

"Ellie, you don't need to do that."

"Do what?"

"Lie. You need some time. It's okay."

"..."

"We can talk about something else if you want."

"Yes, okay. Thanks."

With her sly little monkey face, Alice adds, "So is it true that he's got a big one?"

"Alice! We didn't sleep together. We just kissed."

"But you must have been able to feel his... joystick?"

Facepalm. Alice says joystick and all I can think about is my mother referring to "knowing other men" after my father. It reminds me that I need to talk to her about Christmas dinner.

"I need you on Wednesday at our place for family photos. It's in the contract that the parents be there, too."

"Ugh. What if I don't want to?"

"Impossible. You owe me after inviting Papa to dinner. Remember?"

"Yeah..."

"Oh, and also, I have to tell you that... Maman has a new boyfriend."

"Good grief! Could this day get any weirder?"

"His name is Nicolas. He's twenty-eight. He's our yoga teacher."

Alice throws her fork into the plate of poutine and cries, "Fuck, Maman!"

In poutine veritas, as they say.

#sam_van #monday #couplegoals

[Fancam] Samuel Vanasse (Monday) NEW SONG "The Only One" Minneapolis concert

9,890 views • 2 hours ago

Kayla Fay

5,843 followers

OMG this song is so cute I'm gonna die!!! If you are a romantic like me, it's a must-watch you guys!!!

80 reviews

Charlotte Grondin

This one's a song for **@quinoaforever**. I am dyyyying, it's so good.

Carrissa Milano

This guy is basically the perfect boyfriend. I wish mine would write songs like that.

Lena Lu

Geez, this is cheesy AF. I think I'm gonna puke rainbows and unicorns.

Samantha Blake

Geez, this girl is SOOOOOOO FREAKING LUCKY to have him.

Amélie CB

AWWWWWWWW. The most romantic song in the history of humanity.

Juliette Juliette Juliette

@quinoaforever LOOK AT THIS !!!

June Bug

Wow, this guy is some lover.

Joannie Bégin

I really don't get what he sees in her. The most beige girl ever.

37

Like every time after I spend the evening with Dave, I wake up like I'm being hit in the face with a shovel.

I've barely opened one eye when I twist around to grab my phone to see whether he's written.

Nothing.

Sigh. I have received a bunch of messages from the agency, which I'll read later.

I close my eyes, try to remember the texture of his skin, the smell of his neck, the weight of his hands on my body.

I shiver. I open my eyes.

I immediately feel very, very bad that I'm thinking about Dave three days before Sam is due back. Given the time, he must already be on his way to Ottawa.

I decide to stay in my state of denial a while longer.

The doorbell rings. I automatically get up to go and answer it. I get about twenty packages a week. I know all the delivery people by their first names.

"Mila?!"

This is a surprise. She's standing in front of me impeccably turned out in an athleisure outfit, her long blonde hair in a ponytail, looking fresh and eager.

She looks like she just stepped off the cover of *Femme* magazine.

And I'm in my pajamas, my eyes gluey, bushy hair and it's after 11:30 a.m.

Damn it.

She hands me an extra-large coffee and says, "Crisis management unit, hello."

"Um...hello. What's happened?"

"Uh-oh. Nobody's told you, huh?"

"Told me what?"

Of course, at this point, I panic. I think Sam's been in an accident on his way back from Minneapolis or, worse, that my thing with Dave has come out.

Mila cuts my guesswork short by holding out her phone. She shows me a Facebook post from Elite dated 11:30 p.m. last night.

It reads, "We know all about Ellie's morning routine, but do you know what she does in the evenings?"

In the photo, you can see me with a beer in my hand in the middle of eating a gigantic poutine with peas and bacon. You can see Alice's beer on the table, but not Alice herself. It looks as though I'm alone.

I look at the stats under the post. 4.6K Likes, 300 comments, 900 shares.

It's already gone viral.

"So, about the comments…" Mila says.

I scroll down.

It's a massacre.

In just twelve short hours, I have become the laughingstock of the entire internet.

I get a lot of hate over the fact that I'm eating poutine while I publish healthy recipes and exercise routines. As if I'd made some kind of vow of abstinence and then was found in bed with an entire hockey team.

There are comments that say that I've totally lost it, ha-ha! Or that it must do me good to finally stuff my face. Some people think that it was inevitable, because "you can take the poutine out of the girl, but you can't take the girl out of the poutine."

What?! Others, no less cringeworthy, say I'm a liar and emphasize that they always knew that I was fake and a "bacon eater." There are people who are happy that I've put on weight, and others who hope that I get fat, lol. Some people even say it's an overreaction and that I have the right to do such a thing "from time to time." One inspired person says that it doesn't count, because my poutine includes green vegetables. I see the word "pig" three times, and "self-indulgent" at least ten.

I'll spare you the rest.

According to Mila, I'm also on my way to becoming a meme. She's already seen one or two of my face in close-up, saying things like "If only my boyfriend looked at me the way Ellie looks at her bacon poutine."

I sigh. Invite Mila to come in.

"Malik's the one who sent me," she says. "It's all going to be okay, you'll see."

I roll my eyes and sigh noisily. I wasn't thinking about Malik. Of course he wants to do some damage control to protect my partnership with Karma. And rightly so. It's not looking great, what with the bacon and all.

I put my coffee on the floor and throw myself onto my couch. Mila tries to look encouraging.

"On the bright side, people love the song."

"The song?"

"What planet were you on last night, exactly?"

"Long story."

"The song Sam wrote for you!"

She flips through her phone, waves at me to make

room on the couch and plays the YouTube video.

We see Sam in concert with his band in Minneapolis. He's being filmed on the phone of some girl in the crowd.

"I wrote this song for Ellie, the love of my life," he says. "You're the girl of my dreams, baby." And he starts to play what is probably the sweetest and most romantic song I've ever heard.

Sam is so sexy when he plays the guitar.

"Fuck!"

"You're not happy?" Mila says, surprised. "It's already got 10,000 views."

"Ah. No, I'm super happy. I was just thinking about the photo…"

Another lie.

Mila sits back on her heels. "Jordanne and I have a plan," she says.

"Who?"

"You know, Jordanne Jacques and me. It's not Malik's idea, but he agrees."

"Jordanne Jacques! What does she have to do with my poutine story?"

Jordanne is pretty much the most popular influencer at the moment. She used to work as a model.

She already had a pretty good following on Instagram when she dropped her fashion career to start a workout and travel chain. She now describes herself as an entrepreneur. She has her own underwear and swimwear company, Beyond Swimwear and Intimate. Rumor has it that it's made her extremely rich. Rumor also has it that she retouches all her photos to give herself a big butt and tiny waist. It's true that when you look at her Instagram feed, the proportions of her body are highly improbable.

That said, she must work out like a devil to keep herself in shape. Working out, plus polylactic acid injections in her buttocks, I'll bet.

There's a limit to what you can do with photo retouching.

"Didn't Jordanne kind of stab you in the back?" I say.

"Seb Hadiba? How did you know?"

"Ha, I just guessed. I knew it!"

Mila looks at me as if she a) doesn't think I'm being very sensitive and b) my timing is ill advised.

"Sorry," I say. "So, what's your plan?"

"Well, Malik is going to take care of the public relations and all that, as usual. He also thinks you should put out a post today, have a good laugh about it, and play down the whole business. But the most important thing is that Jordanne wants to collaborate with you on her web series. It features profiles of inspiring people to present her new swimwear collection. We're in a bit of a rush, we're shooting on Tuesday and Wednesday. It's going online this week."

"Since when do you collaborate with Jordanne?"

"It's new. We're trying it out. I'm the artistic director."

I sit up on the sofa and swallow big gulps of coffee. The situation is serious. So much for my caffeine detox. I try to be as upbeat as Mila, but I have the intellectual acuity of a boiled shrimp in the mornings.

"What's the project?" I ask. "What does it involve?"

"They're videos in the form of profiles, where we invite people from different backgrounds to talk about their journey and what inspires them. You said yourself that we 'promote' stereotypes. Well, if you want, now's the time to change that! You can talk about your vision about things. I know it will get people talking. Just take a look at our mood board."

I can't say why, but I get the feeling that Mila is

playing with me right now. I watch her tap the screen of her cell.

"I think that, for you, it would be a great opportunity to bounce back, and to just shine in general."

It's sketchy. I try to buy some time.

"Malik agrees with this?"

"Mmmhmm. Jordanne wants to start the series off with you, because she thinks that you really personify the values of Beyond Swimwear and because you have a really great community."

"I don't know, Mila. I'm not feeling it."

"Ellie, excuse me for saying this, but given what happened yesterday, you're not really in the best position to say no. Look at it as a way of accepting a helping hand."

It's probably because the caffeine has kicked in, but suddenly I understand why Mila has come to my aid.

"That's why you're here, isn't it? Because I can't say no?"

"Well, maybe a little, ha-ha… but no hard feelings, eh?"

She thinks this is funny. I don't get what's in it for her if I participate in this project of Jordanne

277

Jacques', but I decide I'm going to think about it while under the influence of a few liters of coffee.

"Give me some time to think it over," I say.

"No prob! I know we're kidding around, but I have your back. We help each other. That's the plan."

"Mmm."

"You know, you are so lucky to have Sam. I don't have that — a teammate. Except for you, of course."

She gives me her most beautiful smile. I force myself to return it. In spite of all my efforts, it probably looks fake from a million miles away. I remember the expression *Keep your friends close and your enemies closer,* and it suddenly takes on its full meaning with Mila Mongeau.

I walk her to the door and promise I'll get back to her quickly.

I then go to my room and look for my cell.

No message from Dave. I sit at the kitchen island with a notebook and a pen to call Malik. We have to manage the "crisis."

Punching his number, I feel a huge weariness. More than anything, I want to fold myself up in Dave's arms, make love like I've never made love before and then sleep for a century...or two.

Malik picks up after three rings.

"I at least hope that the poutine was good, Élisabeth. Very original, the green peas and bacon. I'll have to try it."

"Y-yes! It's not bad, with the peas…"

It's too many emotions in a short time. I burst into tears.

"But, no, no. It's nothing. Uncle Malik is here. I'll take care of everything, you'll see."

Samuel Vanasse has sent you a Facebook message

S: Change of plan. I'll just make it in time for the Karma photos on Wednesday, but I'll be there, don't worry. X

David Lanctôt has sent you a Facebook message

D: I think about you a lot more often than I should, Quinoa. Send some news.

38

I agreed with Malik that I would go to the agency this morning. Needless to say, I haven't slept all night. It shows in my face, I guess, because Malik is so nice when he sees me. He must think I'm upset because of the now famous photo of me in communion with a poutine.

If he only knew.

"Ellie, before I forget. Karine from Glow just called. She's inviting you to the Post Malone concert in Toronto with the other ambassadors of the Glow from the Inside campaign. She needs a quick response."

"Who are the other ambassadors?"

"Maëla Djeb and...let's see...the little blonde who sounds like she has a cold...Sarah Coutu."

"Hmm...They want stories, I guess? When is it?"

"November twenty-fifth."

"No. Say no. I don't want to send the message that I'm playing in the same leagues as Sarah Coutu or Maëla Djeb. We're aiming higher than that. Tell them it's very nice, but that I already have an engagement to promote the book. Which isn't a lie, anyway."

Malik smiles out of the corners of his lips. It looks

like he approves of my decision. Even better, he looks proud of me.

I'm starting to understand the game. Let's just say I've come a long way since our first meeting a year ago. I think that I'm about to become a not-bad businesswoman. Okay, I realize I'm saying that even though I've just messed up in a major way.

"I'm telling you, Ellie, that what's happened to you is a blessing."

"A blessing?"

"It was high time we dumped this image of you as the perfect girl. Yes, it's brutal, but you'll see that it's a positive thing in the long run. What people want is authenticity. They like things to be a bit untidy. Not too squeaky clean."

"I don't see how being perfect is a problem…"

"Really? So then why is everyone so happy to see you trip up right now?"

I shrug my shoulders.

"Because people are mean."

"No! Because next to you with your parsley smoothies, your yoga routines and all your stuff, people feel inadequate. And now they can take revenge. It was to be expected."

I don't understand why I would have this effect on them. I'm a long way from thinking that I'm better than everyone else.

"But what about Karma? What are they saying?"

"Well, they love you, except they think maybe now isn't the best moment to launch a campaign with you. Not that they disapprove of your actions, but with all the jokes going around, they're worried. They're afraid of being caught up in it."

"Yeah...I understand."

"The brands are always a bit cautious. Totally normal."

To lose Karma, the contract of my dreams, over a silly thing like this...I can't believe it! I've worked so hard. All my recipes, my exclusive videos — in the garbage...and no contract in front of me. Nothing.

It pisses me off. But I think the worst thing is that I know very well that there's only one person to blame, and that's me. If I'd stayed focused on my goals, this never would have happened. I have been the biggest fool of all time.

"But, but..." Malik adds. "I've promised them a Christmas celebration oozing with good feelings. With Sam in the loop, his successful tour, your love that never stops growing, all the potential that you have together, I convinced them that they are going to miss the boat if they pull out now."

"Really? I still have the contract? Oh, my God. Okay, then! I was so worried."

"You're going to have to pull out all the stops, my sweetie. Something nice and cheesy, eh? But vegan! No bacon this time."

Malik thinks he's being funny. But I'm taking this as a serious warning. I almost ruined everything. The Karma photo shoot is in two days and I urgently need Sam. They've bought us as a couple. The perfect love life of a perfect girl.

For two seconds, I imagine what things would be like without him, and I get a bit dizzy. Would I still sell if I were just Ellie? Quinoa without the Forever? Clearly not.

Oh, my God, what was I thinking when I kissed Dave? Am I self-sabotaging? Of course, I did it to hurt myself. That's clear.

Malik brings me back to earth.

"Oh, and Ellie, the project with Jordanne Jacques, that's a yes, right? We're negotiating with her right now. I would like her to join our agency. She is head over heels over you. Help me make her happy, would you?" Jordanne Jacques is head over heels over me? I'm flattered.

"If that would make you happy... It's on Tuesday, right?"

"Tuesday, nine o'clock, Studio Darling. I'll send you an email right away."

"It's starting to look like you planned it, this whole thing," I laugh.

"Not at all! It's a good opportunity, that's all. Go ahead and talk about your bruised self-esteem. Make people cry. Show them the beautiful, endearing and authentic young woman that you are."

"Okay."

"Great. Let's go!"

This is the signal to leave. For the first time, Malik gets up, too, holds out his arms and gives me a hug. Not a sexy hug like Sam or Dave, but a big-brother hug. I'm touched.

Before leaving the office I say, "Malik..."

"What?"

"Thank you."

His face lights up.

"Onward!" he says.

**Top 10 YouTubers
CAN/FR**

1. Jordanne Jacques – 806,100 followers
2. Tellement Cloé – 763,020 followers
3. Cath Bonenfant – 505,300 followers
4. **Ellie - Quinoa Forever – 501,100 followers**
5. Mila Mongeau – 500,800 followers
6. Emma & Juju – 499,900 followers
7. Approved by Gwen – 427,600 followers
8. Sophie Chen – 343,700 followers
9. Maëla Djeb – 162,100 followers
10. Zoé around the World – 144,650 followers

Text messages between Ellie and Alice

E: We start at 4 p.m. on Wednesday. You can't be late. I'm providing supper.

E: And dress like last time, the skirt and the shirt, it was great! See you Wednesday.

A: I hate you.

E: No, you love me. XXX

Text messages between Ellie and Jacques

E: Hi Papa. Still up for the "Christmas" supper on Wednesday?

J: Absolutely!

E: Perfect. They say you should wear neutral colors if poss. Gray, blue or black. No slogans.

E: And I should warn you straight off. Maman has invited her new boyfriend . . .

39

Tuesday, 9:00 a.m.

I show up at Studio Darling as agreed. Jordanne Jacques comes to meet me while Mila is busy arranging the last details of the set. The background she's come up with is colorful and minimalist. I love it. It's beautiful, like everything she touches.

Jordanne is wearing jogging pants and an oversized hoodie. Her hair is pulled up in a loose bun and she's wearing big round glasses but no makeup. I don't even recognize her. Her look almost makes me think of Alice, but the $500 version, say.

Jordanne, I realize pretty quickly, is a girl of few words. She signals to me to follow her and takes me to a rack filled with Beyond Swimwear bikini tops and bottoms in all sizes and colors.

"Pick what you want," she says in an offhand way. "It's a gift."

"Cool, I'll look at them later. Thanks."

There's not much here for me as far as bikinis go. I show off my tummy as seldom as possible.

Jordanne seems to hesitate.

"Oh, but…" she finally says. "Mila didn't tell you?"

She looks over at Mila, but she's in a discussion with someone who seems to be the director. On the set, there's also a cameraman, makeup person and sound engineer. They all look very busy.

On the couches at the back of the studio I see three girls in their twenties, tapping away on their laptops. I assume this is the Beyond Swimwear marketing team or something like that.

Seeing that Mila is not about to come to her aid, Jordanne rustles up her courage and says, "The concept is that you'll be wearing a bathing suit for the interview."

"Oh!...Okay. So, do you have any one-pieces? It's more my style."

"No, we're just making bikinis for now."

Mega vertigo. I come within a hair — just a tiny hair — of walking out. Of telling off Mila and Jordanne and their ridiculous bikini project. But I swallow the urge. Because it's high time I got on top of all this. I've been slacking off lately.

I take a deep breath and pick out a top and bottom that seem to contain a bit more fabric. I slip behind a tiny curtain in a small corner of the studio. Then I move on to makeup. I work hard on sucking in my stomach. If I let go of my abs even for two seconds, my secret bulges will poke out over the bikini bottom. And that would be very embarrassing in front of Mila and Jordanne.

While a nice makeup artist makes me look like I've just had a good night's sleep — something that hasn't happened for three days — I watch Mila on the set. She reacts to the slightest inflection in Jordanne's voice, the slightest lift of her eyebrow, by nodding her head.

After consulting with her team, Jordanne decides she prefers the less stripped-down decor. She'd like more furniture, more accessories. Maybe a few plants?

To my huge surprise, Mila goes along with Jordanne's wishes. She carries out the orders. Obediently.

It takes me back ten years to when Mila was Ariane Brunelle's little lapdog.

And that's when I have a revelation. Mila has always done everything in her power to please girls who are more popular than her. Girls like Ariane Brunelle, like Jordanne Jacques.

Even today, she grovels at her feet.

I know she has way more character than that. If she wanted, Mila could send Jordanne packing and do what she wants. She has the talent for it, and...

It comes as a shock to realize why she participated in the whole salad-in-front-of-my-locker incident. It had nothing to do with me. It was just to look good in Ariane's eyes.

I'm stunned. Poor Mila.

Oops. I just let go of my stomach.

THROWBACK

It's the day before the graduate exhibition. Rumors about the incident are spreading through the school like stomach flu.

Mila's artwork has been vandalized. Some say it was cut into small pieces with a knife. Others say someone punched a hole through it with their fist. I even hear whispers at the lockers that someone stomped on it and threw it in the garbage.

Which is highly unlikely, given the size of the canvas.

When I get to the art room after my French class, Mila is in a complete state. A small posse of girls has clustered around her. They take turns giving her hugs while the most optimistic talk about how they can save the work.

As for me, I go straight to my spot at the back of the room and pretend to work on my pastel portrait of Alice. I go relatively unnoticed. There are a couple of others in the class rushing to finish their work before the exhibition.

Bent over my drawing, I don't miss a word of the discussions going on about the canvas. It's unanimous. It was ruined by an exacto knife. A single straight line from top to bottom. Everyone asks who could have had it in for Mila so badly as to resort to this. Someone who was jealous, that's for sure.

I look up. I realize Mila is looking at me. I hold her gaze and feel all her pain. I return it.

I know that she knows. But she doesn't say anything. Goes back to her flock.

They decide that the canvas can be patched from behind. Mila will still be able to show it. You practically won't be able to tell. Cries of joy. And everyone gets back to work.

She never calls me out. I think that for her it would be like admitting defeat. Becoming a victim in the eyes of the world. And anyway, why direct any of the attention away from herself?

At the exhibition, the work is a resounding success. The whole school comes out in solidarity to see the magnificent work that has been mutilated and then valiantly repaired.

But once again, it's Mila we admire, who we love. Mila who floats like a feather in a beautiful world. Mila who's so fuckin' special.

And with all this love, there's nothing left for the Ellies of this world.

40

After a good half hour of back and forth between the Beyond Swimwear team and Mila on which adjustments to make to the set, we're finally ready to shoot.

Mila makes me sit on a kind of high stool. I have to make a big effort to keep my legs slightly elevated, otherwise my thighs will spread on the seat and that would be horrible. Someone powders my nose before Jordanne sits behind the camera with the whole team.

Mila explains a bit about what's going to happen.

"So our series is called Body Positive, and the aim is to show that no matter what kind of body you have, it's important to feel beautiful on the inside, because it's our differences that make us magnificent. You know what I mean?"

I'm wondering how sixteen-year-old Ellie would feel listening to this come out of the mouth of a girl like Mila, like Jordanne or like...me. That the important thing is to feel beautiful on the inside.

I think that sixteen-year-old Ellie would never have believed it, that what was on the inside, or that being different, would be "magnificent" to others.

She wouldn't have listened to any of this. I think she would have especially noticed the bodies of these girls. Their "perfect" bodies. Their retouched, submissive bodies. Reproduced a thousand times. A body like a siren. A message. An injunction to conform, to obey.

And I realize that I have betrayed her, that sixteen-year-old Ellie. I have been part of it.

I feel dizzy. Someone turns on the camera. It starts to roll.

I should have listened to my little voice. I should have really listened and turned down the project.

"Jordanne will ask you some questions," Mila continues, "but we won't hear them on the video. You'll have to reformulate them for the camera before answering. Is that okay with you?"

I nod. Jordanne flips through her papers. She seems nervous. Almost intimidated.

"Sorry, this is the first time I've done this," she says.

I smile at her honesty. My stomach relaxes a little. I try to suck it in with all my strength.

"First question," Jordanne says. "How did you learn to love your body?"

PURSUE WHAT IS PRETTY

You want to scream that you're not feeling well. That they told you a big lie. That it doesn't make you happy. Being thin. Being beautiful. That you always have to start again. That it's never enough. That it's ridiculous. The mold. Fitting into it.

You want to say something true. You'd like to speak up. Get away from the phrases you've repeated a hundred times.

But you don't succeed. Because everything around you is so fucking beautiful. The smiling faces. The slim bodies. Exciting collaborations. The turquoise water. It's so turquoise. Your background, your lighting, your makeup, your lip injections, your outfit.

It all swallows you up. You are swallowed up by the beauty. You can say anything at all, you can write what you want in the captions, but no one will listen. The message won't get through. It's been swallowed up. Empty.

And you're stuck. Trapped by the illusion that you yourself have created. That is feeding you because you can't do otherwise. The force is too strong.

And the water is so turquoise.

41

The first thing that surprises me when Sam arrives at the apartment is that I am truly glad to see him. I thought a feeling of remorse would take the upper hand, but no.

I forgot how handsome he is. When Sam walks into the room, you just cannot look anywhere else.

"I'm back!"

"Yay, at last!"

In a naive attempt to get back to normal, I fling myself around his neck.

"Thanks for the song! I've listened to it three thousand times this week. It is so sweet!"

I kiss him. Sam returns my kiss, but no more. He plants me coldly back on the ground like he's putting a book back on the table.

He pulls away then to say hello to the team from Karma. I introduce Joëlle and Carolina, who are putting the final touches on the dishes in the kitchen.

He waves to Bianca, whom he amuses by calling her our official photographer. She's setting up some lights in the living room, which has become a grand holiday dining room since this morning. I hid the couch and TV in the guest room slash office slash storage room. It was no picnic but I had help from the Karma team.

They've thought of everything — logistics, the groceries, our outfits, the decor. There are even presents under the tree.

Okay, empty boxes beautifully wrapped, but still.

I tell Sam that he has to change because my family will be arriving in fifteen minutes.

He follows me into the bedroom. I close the door. He drops his bag on the bed.

"Everything okay?" I ask quietly.

"Just average."

"What's happening?"

He sits calmly on the bed, clasps his hands together.

"Can we talk about what happened after I left?"

I have a punch of guilt in the pit of my stomach.

Dave. Sam knows about Dave.

Oh, no. Shit, shit, shit…

He's talking in almost a whisper so no one can hear.

"A poutine and a beer…in public? What were you thinking, Ellie?"

I freeze.

"What's wrong with you?" he says. "You're not like before. It's like you're letting yourself go... Like what we're building together isn't important."

"Are you kidding me? You're not serious, Sam."

Sam asks me to lower my voice. Then he gets up and starts to empty his suitcase onto the bed, throwing his running shoes into the closet before continuing, somehow trying to whisper.

"Everything I do is always for the two of us, okay? I break my ass composing a fucking romantic song for you, while meanwhile, you blow the image that we've been working to build with Malik. What the fuck, Ellic?"

"But what are you talking about? I have the right to eat a poutine with my sister if I want! As far as I know, you've never been deprived of doing anything. Plus, I hadn't eaten anything all day, for your information!"

"Okay, but did you really have to do it in public? In front of the whole world? I can't believe you are so lacking in judgment. Geez."

"Agh, so I made a mistake. It happens! Are you really going to stick my nose in it? I'm not entitled to even a small 'Poor you, are you okay?' Really?"

"Look, Ellie, you're not five years old. You're old enough to assume responsibility for your actions."

"Excuse me?! I —"

Sam signals that he's heard enough. It kills me. As much as I'm the first to blame myself for the poutine incident, coming from him, I find this completely unfair.

"Why don't you tell me what's really bothering you, eh? That you met a lot of hot girls on tour and that you miss your life as a fucking rock star, and you're disappointed to have to come home and find me here because I'm just ordinary next to your pack of groupies in heat."

It's fascinating, the things that go through your head during a fight. As if, apart from a certain degree of emotional instability, we also have the gift of clairvoyance.

Sam throws his clothes into the laundry basket.

"You'll say anything right now —"

"Okay, so first of all, what's the problem? It bugs you that I ate a poutine because you think I'm 'letting myself go'? Is that it?"

". . ."

"Tell me!"

"Oh, forget it. You're just going to freak out again."

"Try me!"

Sam gives a long sigh. He sits back on the bed. There's an eternal silence, during which I hear my mother and Nico arrive. Shit. They greet the whole team. My mother marvels over the Christmas decorations. Asks if she's suitably dressed. Says that she has options if she needs to change.

As for Nico, he introduces himself to everyone. He thinks it smells super good in here.

I'd like to go out to greet them so things aren't quite so weird, but it's impossible.

Sam finally decides to speak.

"Okay...sometimes, I'm scared."

"..."

"I'm afraid that...never mind."

"Oh, come on, Sam!"

"I'm afraid that you'll go back to the way you were before."

"..."

"..."

"That I'll put on the weight I lost? Is that it?"

301

"Yes."

I want to cry. I'm sure I'm going to cry.

"You're a real asshole," I say.

Sam is stricken. He's hurt.

"That will teach me to show that I care and write romantic songs for you."

He's talking too loud, and I signal to him to turn down the volume.

"Agh, fuck you with your romantic song, okay?" I say. "You didn't return a single message during the whole tour! Even when I wrote that I wasn't feeling all that great. In fact, don't come and make like you care just because you wrote a song! We both know what it is. This 'song' is nothing more than a publicity stunt. That's the only thing you care about. You don't give a shit how I feel. Fact is, you take me for a complete fool!"

Carolina knocks on the door to let us know that my mother has arrived. Sam takes off his T-shirt and pulls on a shirt.

"What am I to you, Ellie?" he says as he buttons it up.

"..."

"Do you ever think for two seconds about what

302

I want? About what would be good for me?"

"..."

"Of course not. Don't do the same thing. Don't take me for a fool. The truth is, you're not on my team, Ellie, and you haven't been for a while."

I surreptitiously wipe the corners of my eyes.

I have to admit that Sam is right. I haven't thought about him a lot lately. Not at all, in fact. I've been thinking about Dave. I remember our kisses and I am completely filled with guilt.

Sam is right. I've let myself go completely. I've dropped the ball.

I hate myself. I had everything I wanted in life, and then I found a way to wreck it all.

I try to hold back a flood of tears.

"I'm going to tell them that we can't —"

"No, no. Out there, we're going to put on our most beautiful smiles, we're going to stop arguing, and Karma is going to get their money's worth, okay?"

I burst into tears.

"You're not going to leave me?" I ask, pitifully.

"Well, no, Ellie, I'm not going to leave you... It's going to be all right, okay? I've got you. I love you! You're my queen!"

"But I've ruined everything…"

"It's all going to work out. You'll see. It will all work out."

Sam's eyes are watery, too. He holds my face in his hands. It shakes me up to see him like this. I wipe my face.

"Okay, I'm coming," I say, sniffling. "Give me five minutes."

He kisses me on the forehead and leaves the room, taking care to close the door behind him. I hear him greet my mother, happy and relaxed. I don't know how he does that.

"Estelle! Always a pleasure to see the most beautiful woman south of the fifty-sixth parallel."

I take off my yoga pants and grab the dress on my bed. It was the "suggestion" of the Karma team. A dress with gold sequins. I pull it up from my feet. Sigh. I squirm as I try to pull the zipper up my back. It doesn't budge.

The dress is small. Too small. I make every effort in the world to compress my ribcage and empty my lungs of air. To stop breathing.

It doesn't budge.

I take off the dress.

I pull on a pair of Spanx. Put on the dress again. With one hand, I try to bring the two sides of the zip closer together, while with the other I desperately pull the zip to the top. I managed to gain two small centimeters, but that's all.

The dress is still open behind my back, from my kidneys to the back of my neck. I'm afraid I'll rip it if I pull any harder.

I imagine going to tell Joëlle and Carolina that the dress is too small. Humiliating.

I decide to put on a small black jacket over it to hide the back opening. The problem won't be visible, but I'll know. I'll know that I am too big to wear my Christmas dress.

I stand in front of the mirror to arrange my face. I touch up my concealer and powder. I thank heaven for the waterproof mascara, and I put on a little lip gloss.

My hand trembles. You can tell I've been crying. I wonder how long I'm going to have to stay hidden in my bedroom before I look normal. I wonder whether Sam really still loves me...

I hear my father arriving with Alice. He also says how good things smell.

I have to go out there. I can't stay hidden in here.

I look myself right in the eyes and say softly, "Shut up, little voice. Shut your trap."

CELEBRITY WORLD

Ellie from Quinoa Forever opens up about her complicated relationship with her body and it's REALLY inspiring

The girlfriend of singer Samuel Vanasse puts on a bikini in the brand-new web series by Jordanne Jacques and shares a message of self-acceptance. We thank her for being so authentic and for inspiring us this way! To see the new Beyond Swimwear swimsuits . . .

We love the new collection of cushions and bedding by Mila Mongeau in collaboration with XY Home

We never get tired of the surprising collaboration between Mila Mongeau and XY Home! At the start of the year, the YouTuber-influencer-Instagrammer launched a home decorating collection to die for. The line is now completely sold out, and we can't wait to see what new pieces will emerge from this beautiful partnership . . .

Annette Bédard poses naked and pregnant (with twins!) on the cover of *Femme* magazine

Isn't she resplendent?! Annette Bédard is pleased to show us her beautiful pregnant belly on the cover of November's *Femme* magazine. The photos are accompanied by a fascinating interview where she reveals that she "feels good with curves" and "more like a woman than ever." This beauty also reveals that she would like to have a third child "around the age of 45 or 46"...

42

Carolina and Joëlle from the Karma team explain how the evening will run. They'll have to take mood shots, portraits, but also — and this is very important — close-ups of the food. Which is why we have to wait for their signal before we eat.

Alice rolls her eyes when Bianca, the photographer, thanks us "in advance" for our patience and asks us to act as natural as possible. I know Alice has made a big effort to be here, so I make a heart sign with my hands from the other end of the table and mouth to her that I love her.

We've barely received permission to start in on the watercress and hemp soup when Sam decides to ask my mother how she and Nico met. Sometimes I can't believe his lack of sensitivity. Like he is simply incapable of putting himself in the place of others.

I hear the clicking of Bianca's camera. I glance over at my father. He seems to be taking it well. For the moment.

"Ah, well," my mother says, her voice full of honey. "Nicolas was my yoga teacher. We flirted with each other for a few months, then we had several 'secret dates,' a few moments of doubt — which is normal — and now he gives me private lessons at home. If you know what I mean."

My mother winks the most uncomfortable wink in the history of humanity.

Sam finds it very funny. Nico looks embarrassed and my father seems to think it's amusing. I think that's very cool of him.

You need to know that my father left my mother for another woman about eight years ago. Her name is Lise-Anne, she was his colleague at work. Classic story. It started with a little hanky-panky at the office party and ended in a bitter divorce. And even if his relationship with Lise-Anne was a resounding failure, my father never stopped feeling guilty for leaving. My sister says he tried to win back my mother after, but she sent him packing. Fair enough.

He raises his glass and says, "To you both, Estelle and Nico!"

At the other end of the table, Alice pours herself a gigantic glass of red wine. She doesn't speak, but her face says it all.

"I'm curious, Nico," Sam asks. "Have you always

been attracted to women with experience, or is it a new thing?"

I widen my eyes at Sam so he understands that he needs to change the subject. Nico puts down his fork.

"Good question, Sam," he says. "I would say that I am never attached to the external bodily shell of my partners. What's important to me is the essence of a person. Estelle and I resonate with each other. We resonate a lot."

My mother bursts out laughing. A long, ecstatic laugh. It's embarrassing.

My father is a good sport and laughs along, too. Alice swallows down her glass of wine, expels a little burp and decides to join in the discussion.

"Don't you find it strange, Estelle, to think that when you were twenty years old, Nico wasn't even born? Like, he could have gone to daycare with Ellie. There's just three years' difference between them."

This makes no impression on my mother.

"Indeed, Alice, I had your sister when I was quite young —"

"That's not my point, Estelle."

I try to intervene before the conversation degenerates.

"Hey, I know it's Halloween tomorrow, but Merry Christmas, everyone. Thank you for being —"

My glass is still in the air when my mother launches her counterattack.

"It's funny, Alice. I thought you and your roommates were such grand feminists."

I notice that her lips are a bit purply from the wine. I think about the photos. They'll have to be retouched.

Alice replies disdainfully, "I don't see the connection between —"

"Oh no? Your sister was telling me that you're going out with one of your sociology professors."

"I don't see the connection."

"Well, a university professor who sleeps with his student is still a brilliant pedagogue in your eyes. But your mother, who had only previously known men who didn't even know what a clitoris —"

I hear my father cough into his soup.

"…and who decides to enjoy herself a bit before her breasts drop below her knees — she's nothing but an old bitch, is that right?"

43

Joëlle and Carolina arrive with the appetizer. Fake fondues in a flax and walnut crust, with a fresh spinach and green apple salad.

I decide to turn the discussion to my creative process. I give plenty of useless details about my recipes. I talk for a very, very long time. I make it impossible for anyone else to get a word in edgewise until they all calm down big time.

Then, around the time of the main course — a roast with lentils, pistachios and sweet potatoes — everyone's attention breaks up, and conversations continue in groups of two.

While we eat, Alice and my father discuss the future of humanity.

As for my mother, she just seems thrilled to be photographed on the arm of Nico. She completely ignores my father. It's perfect that way.

Sam whispers a few words in my ear. Tells me that he loves me, that I'm beautiful, and that he's bored. It makes me blush. Bianca can take advantage of the moment to photograph us. We laugh, we kiss. I tell myself that I can't wait to see the photos and that at least I am super proud of my recipes. The girls from Karma have executed them to perfection.

But at dessert, coming out of sweet nowhere, my mother decides to ask my father about the state of his health while Bianca immortalizes my cocoa, hazelnut and honeysuckle cake sitting in the middle of the table.

"So, Jacques," she says. "Are you better? Were they able to get rid of your little tumors?"

She's holding Nico's hand in full view on the table to let my father know that while he may have health problems, she is sexually active with a twenty-eight-year-old yogi.

My father's eyes don't leave his plate.

"Yes. But... I'm afraid that... the tests have revealed... it's cancer. The masses are cancerous. They think other organs may be affected. I see my doctor next week to discuss possible treatments."

My mother stiffens. Nico looks like he wants to disappear. Alice drops her fork onto her plate.

In a last-ditch effort to break the uneasy mood he's created, my father takes on his philosophical manner, which has always annoyed me the most.

"But as the greatest Russian romantic novelist wrote, 'To live without hope is to cease to live.'"

Sam immediately raises his glass.

"To hope! And to Jacques!" he says, his face beaming.

My mother does the same. I see Sam and my mother strike a pose and smile. Bianca moves quickly around us, taking dozens of photos a minute. It makes me dizzy.

I make a big effort to smile, too. Alice looks completely disoriented.

My father and I exchange glances. His eyes too blue. His face frozen in a pained smile. Terrified at the idea of his own mortality.

Bianca quietly informs us that she has finished. That she has everything she needs. The team starts to wrap up. Sam stops smiling. He puts down his glass.

Alice stands up, throws her napkin onto her plate and goes to the bathroom to cry. My mother looks away. Nico stares down at his plate.

But I just watch my father.

He looks so small. So harmless. I wish I could love him. I wish it were possible.

The silence has become unbearable.

"It's going to be okay," I say. "We're here for you, Papa."

But I'm lying. Christmas in October. The empty boxes under the fir tree. Alice in a skirt. My living room turned into a dining room. The rented furniture. A dress that won't do up. My mother on the arm of her trophy boyfriend. Sam who always turns off at the same time as the cameras. A tiny, not-dead father.

Ellie and Sam's Vegan Christmas.

The most beautiful lie of all.

44

Everybody has left. I tell Sam I'm going to keep Alice company. Cheer her up.

I leave him tidying up the living room by himself. I take off my dress, put on jeans and a cotton hoodie and boots, and go out into the cold October air.

I take a deep breath. I walk and walk until I get to the corner of Laurier and St-André. I pray hard that he'll be there. But the Closed sign is on the door of the café.

I'm getting ready to move to Plan B and go to Alice's, when I see a light on inside. I knock.

Dave comes to open the door, a beige-gray paint roller in his hand.

I point to the roller.

"Mystical Taupe?"

He thinks about it a bit.

"June Mist," he says.

"Good choice."

"You took your time, Quinoa."

45

Dave lives fifteen minutes from the café, in a small, fairly cute apartment on the second floor of a duplex. I feel like I've lived here in another life.

He asks if I'm hungry. I say yes. That I'm dying of hunger. He announces that he's going to prepare his specialty, macaroni and orange cheese. I smile, but not a lot. I think he guesses I'm feeling messed up.

While Dave cooks the pasta I hardly say a word. He looks like he's wondering what kind of strange creature has just landed in his kitchen. I realize that we know each other but not really.

He drains the pot and rummages around in the fridge. He pulls out a carton of cream and a pound of butter.

"You're not going to put in cream!"

"Better than milk."

I think about Josiane. Her big, enthusiastic eyes. Her spandex. Then I mentally send her for a walk.

I sit on the counter. I never do that. It does me good to not be that person. Someone who never sits on the counter. It's like a new start.

"I'm *so* sorry. I really don't have any spinach or

green stuff to put in to make up for my sins."

"If you want my opinion, you're going straight to hell."

Dave adds butter to the yellowy-orange mixture and says, "Anyway, I heard that hell was full of girls who say brezel instead of pretzel...Wouldn't want to go anywhere else."

I blush.

"Brezel. Brezel. Brezel," I say softly.

Dave comes over to me. Our noses are the same height. I look into his eyes.

I get the feeling that he knows everything. That he sees everything. That he can take everything.

It gets stronger, too strong, and I kiss him.

Dave understands everything about kissing. Lots of lips, not too much tongue. It's gentle and sweet and I'm floating. He lifts my hoodie up over my head. I hesitate.

After this, I can't go back...but I miss Dave, and I can't resist any longer. I take off his sweater and my bra.

His skin on my skin. I'm melting. He lifts me off the counter and sets me down on the table.

"Kitchen tables, totally overrated," I say. "Hurts

the tailbone. The bed, please?"

He laughs. We walk to his bedroom half naked. I feel like I'm twelve years old. Except that we're making love.

It's too bright in the room. I'm having a hard time letting go. It's not like with Sam. When Sam makes love with me it's like an athletic performance. Like a kind of porn film.

With Dave it's different. It's gentle but almost awkward. I try to...participate. I've forgotten how to do it. I just know what Sam likes. Like a choreography I know by heart. A choreography that seems completely ridiculous to me now that I'm performing without him.

Dave asks whether there's a position I prefer. I don't know. I don't know what I like. I like it when the other person likes it. I am such a loser. I tell him not to wait for me. That I won't have an orgasm, that I never do the first time. It's always such a disappointing moment to say that.

Dave finishes. He kisses me and lies beside me.

"Wow. That was terrible," he says after about three full minutes.

He laughs. I laugh.

"We failed! We failed sex." I cover my face with my hand.

He kisses me on the cheek.

"But we didn't fail the rest of it. I'm happy you're here, Quinoa."

"I'm happy, too."

"We're going to have to keep practicing."

I put on one of his T-shirts and go to the bath-room to have a pee. Looking at myself in the mirror, I check in with my little voice. I go back to the bedroom.

"Is it okay if I sleep here?"

"Of course."

"But you would tell me if you preferred that I go, promise?"

"The truth..."

"..."

"The truth is that I want you to stay."

We eat the macaroni straight from the pot. It's delicious. We do the dishes. We go to bed naked and talk all night. He holds me in his arms. I think I have never felt so good with someone. His way of touching me...It's chemistry, I think.

Around 3:00 a.m., we make love again. It's not like

the first time. It's better. A lot better.

And I fall asleep. Deeply.

46

8:42 a.m. Like I've done this a thousand times, I get out of bed without waking Dave, put on my clothes and sneak out of the apartment. I jump into a taxi to get back home. I pray that Sam is still sleeping.

I'm trying to think of two or three believable things that I can tell him about my night at Alice's. I hope I'll have time to take a shower before he wakes up.

I slip my key in the lock. I turn the handle very slowly. I hang up my bag. I bend down to take off my boots.

When I look up, Sam is in front of me in the hallway. He looks feverish. He's holding a selfie stick in his hands. His phone is at the end.

Sneaking looks at the screen, he takes me by the hand and pulls me into the living room.

I laugh, but I'm 100 percent nervous.

"Sam, what are you doing?"

"We're live on YouTube, my love!"

"Okay...Good morning, YouTube."

"Because...Ellie."

Without letting go of his selfie stick, Sam kneels

down and checks that we are in the frame.

"Yes?"

"Without you, nothing works. Nothing makes sense. You are my rock, Ellie. I love you."

He puts one hand in his pocket and takes out a small turquoise box.

I tell myself that I must absolutely control my face. That it's not what I think it is.

I wonder how many people are watching this right now.

I smile because that is my only option.

Sam looks at me as he tries to open the box with his free hand.

"Élisabeth Bourdon-Marois, will you marry me?"

#GRATITUDE

The author would like to thank Olivier, Joëlle, Martin and Christine for their support and invaluable contributions while writing this novel. She also thanks the whole Café Lézard team for the 461 cappuccinos and 128 burritos that were needed to complete this project.

LAURENCE BEAUDOIN-MASSE has written two novels: *Suck It In and Smile* (originally published as *Rentrer son ventre et sourire*) and its sequel. She is a concept editor for Radio-Canada. Laurence would like to help girls who, like her, never feel that they measure up. She lives in Montreal, Quebec.

SHELLEY TANAKA is an award-winning author, translator and editor who has written and translated more than thirty books. She teaches at Vermont College of Fine Arts. Shelley lives in Kingston, Ontario.